Advance Praise for

MY OLD FAITHFUL

"Yang Huang's collection of linked stories peels back the layers of a culture too often rendered exotic and opaque to reveal what is intimate and familiar. Sexual awakenings, sibling rivalries, the pain and joy of raising children, aging, the constraints of love and loyalty are all dealt here with a gentle and incisive hand. *My Old Faithful* is a deeply moving portrait of a family and a society."
—Hasanthika Sirisena, author of *The Other One*

"In *My Old Faithful,* Yang Huang explores with humor, tenderness and fierce precision the ties that bind separate a family across time and space. Fil¹ unexpected turns and a painterly attention is a wise and beautiful book."
—Elizabeth Graver, author of *T*

MY OLD FAITHFUL

Also by Yang Huang
Living Treasures

MY OLD FAITHFUL

Stories

YANG HUANG

UNIVERSITY OF MASSACHUSETTS PRESS
Amherst and Boston

ISBN 978-1-62534-336-9 (paper)

Designed by Sally Nichols
Set in Adobe Garamond Pro
Printed and bound by Maple Press, Inc

Cover design by Kristina Kachele Design, llc
Cover art: Lovesiyu, *Peony* © 123RF.com

Library of Congress Cataloging-in-Publication Data
A catalog record for this book is available from the Library of Congress.

British Library Cataloguing-in-Publication Data
A catalog record for this book is available from the British Library.

Reference material in "The Birthday Girls" from *Bodhisattva of Compassion*
by John Blofeld. Courtesy of Shambhala Publications.

To my parents, for your love.
And to Qin, for your steadfast support.

CONTENTS

CONTENTS

THE WOMEN IN LOVE

MY OLD FAITHFUL

THE SELFISH YOUNGSTERS

子—What the Son Did . . .

PINING YELLOW

"Are you comfy down there, son?" Mom asked.

I grabbed my bowl from the floor to stuff a chopstick-load of rice into my mouth so that I couldn't talk. I saw Mom's knees open and her elbows slip back. I was relieved she didn't poke her head under the dining table to spy on me.

"You can bark for a yes," she said.

So I woofed twice and stuck out my tongue, like my dog Yellow.

"Let me give you some pork ribs," she said.

I put my bowl in her hand and scooted out of her sight. I'd been eating my suppers under the table ever since Yellow disappeared two weeks ago. Dad said Yellow had been trapped by thieves and then eaten, though no one knew that for sure. I wanted to be the first to spot Yellow when he hopped over our doorstep again, but he never did, so I disappeared, too, and got into hiding with him.

Mom passed me back the bowl. "Finish it off, son. Yellow will want that."

I used to feed Yellow my pork ribs and loved to hear him chew the bones with a loud crunching sound. After a big meal, I would've kicked off my shoes to straddle his back, his tail wagging behind my butt. He would've carried me to his rattan bed, while we yelped at each other like Labrador brothers.

Dad had brought Yellow home two years ago in a tote bag. There was a ripe apple at the bottom of his tote bag. Yellow rested on the apple, his eyes shut with puffy eyelids. His cream coat became pure gold when it caught the light, so I called him Yellow. Yellow weighed thirty-five kilos when he last stood on the scale at the meat market.

I spat the chewed bone into my bowl. The fatty marrow made me nauseated. "Why did anyone want to eat my Yellow?" I asked.

"Because they're jealous," Dad said. "It isn't good for a dog to be so gorgeous in our neighborhood."

"Why?"

"Yellow carried himself like a wolf, so the thieves wanted to sink their teeth into his brawn. People aren't mean to just dogs—this lousy luck also goes for the fattest pig in the sty."

I wiped my eyes with my sleeve and tried not to make a sound when I cried. Why did the thieves take the whole Yellow? I might've been less mad if they had left me a piece of him, a bone or a tooth to remember him by. I could never forget Yellow, but every day his face became more blurred in my mind.

I could only hide under the table as we had done when we were pups together. Mom stood up to get Dad more rice. When her chair slid back and made a loud noise, I threw a bone on the floor and crawled on my hands and knees to pick it up with my teeth, like Yellow would have.

On my way to school I stopped by the dough figurine booth. The candy man liked to holler at children who didn't have money, so I had never bothered to look through the figurines when Yellow was with me. The man must've been even older than my dad, because he had a white beard, but my dad didn't have a pair of magical hands like his. The old man kneaded colored sugar dough into figurines like Monkey King and Pigsy, and blew into a bamboo stick to make their knickerbockers expand like lanterns. Then he glazed the figurines with syrup and stuck them on a straw mast. I stood on my tiptoes to gaze at them.

"Do you want one, little brother?" the man asked me.

"My dad doesn't allow it," I said.

"Then you'd better hurry away to school. Get lost!"

I reached out to turn the figurine around to admire the details of Monkey King. Dad had said the candy was dirty because the man blew into it with his mouth, and the glue he used in the dough was unhealthy. But there were plenty of other children who weren't afraid of germs or glue. The man stuck a whistle with red and white stripes onto the mast.

"Can I blow it?" I asked.

He opened his hand at me. "Fifty cents and it's all yours."

"It only takes a second."

He beat away my hand that hovered over the mast. "Are you asking others to eat your germs?" he scolded.

I thrust my fists into my pockets and swung my backpack sideways. School would start in a few minutes, but I wasn't worried about that. I stood on my tiptoes to sniff at the whistle. It smelt lightly of licorice, like bubble gum. I didn't have a sweet tooth, but this was a special candy. An idea popped into my head.

"Can you make a dog? A two-year-and-two-month-old yellow Labrador?"

"What's it like?" He stared at me over the rim of his specs.

I held out my hand with palm down. Yellow would've trotted over to stand under my hand if I hadn't lost him. "It's about a half meter tall and weighs thirty-five kilos. It's the strongest Labrador you've ever seen. Yellow has Irish Setter in his blood, so he's a super Retriever with a glossy coat and hazel eyes."

The man interrupted me, "Two yuan."

"Why is it so—?"

"Because it's custom-made. Do you know what that means, kid? Bring me a picture of your dog, and I'll make one just like him from ear to tail. Tell you what, I'll throw in a nametag for free, how's that?" I backed off when he yelled in my face, "What is two yuan to you, a month's allowance?"

My parents wouldn't give us allowances until we turned ten years old. Mom had said we couldn't be wasteful like some families because there were three of us children. My older sister was nine, I was seven, and my younger sister was only four. I let Mom deposit my red envelope money from my grandparents into our family bank. The New Year was in February, but I couldn't wait to have my Yellow figurine.

"If I pay you two yuan, you have to make Yellow a wagging tail. I want one with fur."

"Two and half yuan."

A girl waving a five-yuan bill jostled me aside. I wished I could've told the old man not to rip me off, but I didn't dare to make him angrier, when he was the only one who could make Yellow for me to hold in my hand. As the man counted the girl's change, I pulled out the whistle to stick it on the side of the straw mast where the old man couldn't see it.

The girl said, "Yummy," and licked the white sleeve of Moon Lady.

"Is it?" I asked.

She peered at me out of the corner of her eye, as if no answer was needed for such a dumb question. When she left, I picked up the whistle from the mast to slide it into my coat sleeve and walked away with her. After we turned the corner, I took out my whistle to blow it.

The girl's eyes popped in amazement. "Where did you get that?"

"Forget it. I won't trade for your Moon Lady."

"Who said anything about trading?" She held up the hand-less Lady that stuck to a few of her long hairs. "How did you buy it so fast?"

I ignored her and blew my whistle so loud that people turned their heads to look. The sugar dough tasted like bubble gum mixed with clay.

"Is it good?" the girl asked.

I chewed off a bite, and the whistle was done for, so I tossed it in the shrubs. I couldn't believe it was worth fifty cents. Outside the school wall, I heard the bell ring and started running, the pencil box rattling in my backpack.

"Oh, it's the school bell!" the girl screeched behind me.

After school my older sister and I walked to the enclosing wall of the park. We had to climb the wall because we didn't have money for the entrance fee. Fortunately my sister was a lot taller than me. She bent down to let me kneel on her back and climb onto the wall. Then I lay on my stomach to pull her up. She stepped on the pattern bricks of the window lattice and grabbed my hand hard. Finally we sat straddling the wall, panting and smiling at each other.

"This isn't so bad," she said.

"I told you! And it's only getting better." I swung my leg aside to face the park. "I dare you to jump!" Then I landed on the soft quilt of pine needles. She hesitated. I waved at her with both hands. "Do it, quick! People outside are watching you!"

She opened her arms to drop off the wall. "Are they coming after us?" She squatted on the pine needles.

"No, you did good. We can go now."

"Yay!" she shouted and sprinted to join the tourists. The river wound a silver belt along the road, darting bright stars in my eyes. I recalled the saying we had learned in school: the autumn sky is clear and the air is bracing. "We've struck gold!" My sister pointed at a pyramid of flowers straight ahead. "It's the Chrysanthemum Show!"

A scent sweeter than the candy I had tasted that morning greeted us as we neared the carpet of mums. Yellow and I would've had fun chasing butterflies in this sea of blossoms. Without him, I didn't have enough eyes to look around me. My sister talked to a woman who was painting a mum.

"That is so pretty, Miss Wu," she said.

"Thank you." Miss Wu rubbed the ink stick on the stone,

then dipped her brush-tip into the ink pool. "Who's that cute boy with you?"

"He's my brother Wei." My sister told me, "Miss Wu is my art teacher. Her traditional Chinese paintings have won prizes for our school."

"Don't boast for me." Miss Wu pressed her brush onto the paper, twisting this way and that to draw the stem and twigs of the mum. "I've been hooked on this species for three days and have done half a dozen paintings. The only thing I'm not crazy about is its name, Yellow Supreme. Does that tell you anything you can't see?"

I pushed to the front to gaze at the mum. Its petals shot out from the core and curved into fishhook tips, and they were pure gold.

Miss Wu lifted her brush and wrote two words, Pining Yellow.

"What does that mean?" my sister asked.

"Pining means wanting," Miss Wu said. "Look at that spider bloom. Why does it have to be so enchanting? It wants something. What do you think it wants?"

"Yellow?" I said.

Miss Wu pointed her brush at me. "You're a bright boy." She smeared leaves onto the branches, then added veins to their smooth surfaces.

I touched her easel, and on it was the most beautiful painting I had ever seen. "Why is it black and white?" I asked.

"And gray." She smiled at me, her lips red and pretty. "You know the answer, because. . . ."

"It wants Yellow," I said.

She nodded. "Yellow is missing because my paintbrush cannot capture its true color. Why fake it, then?" She tapped my hand with the end of her brush.

I stepped forward to pick up the mum pot. It was heavier than it looked.

"What are you doing?" Miss Wu asked. "Put it down, or a park employee will catch you for stealing."

"I want to see if they look alike."

Miss Wu sighed and got up to take my mum pot. "I love traditional painting because it's a pure expression. Copying is boring, don't you think?" She took the paper from the easel to roll it up. "I would love to paint a whole book of this species. Too bad the show will end on Friday, and I cannot buy the pot."

"Why not?" my sister asked.

"The good ones are not on sale, because the park keeps them to breed new plants." She sliced at a stem with her palm. "You know, you can cut off a branch to grow a new plant."

"Any twig?" I asked.

"Pretty much."

I ran off to the sales section. Most of the pots were priced between five to ten yuan. Since Pining Yellow was a good one, it must have been worth at least five yuan. If I grew a pot for Miss Wu, she'd pay me enough money to buy a Yellow figurine. Miss Wu was still talking to my sister, when I snuck behind Pining Yellow to snap off a branch and peeled a stripe of skin off my twig. No one noticed me sliding it into my pocket, so I decided not to tell my sister about it until I raised a mum.

We got home and I sprinted for the yard. The hens were striding around me, as I dug a hole to put in the twig. I was stamping the loose dirt around the mum, when my younger sister came to call me for supper. She saw the shovel in my hand.

"What're you doing with that?" she asked.

"Mind your own business."

I marched to the dining table to take my old seat. My parents stared at my face as if I had grown a beard.

My sister chirped, "Older Brother buried something in the yard."

Mom hushed her.

"What did you bury?" Dad asked.

I plied rice into my mouth and chewed on it for some time, but the whole table was waiting for me to talk, so I gulped a spoonful of bean thread soup to wash down my food.

"I was just playing with my shovel," I said with a slurp.

Mom burst into a smile. "The food is hot, son, chew slowly." She scooped chunks of meat and fish into my bowl and then said to Dad, "Do you care for a drink, old man? Our son is back."

I couldn't finish the food that Mom piled in my bowl, so I gave some to my older sister.

"We struck gold today, didn't we?" she whispered to me.

"What did you do?" my younger sister asked.

"Eat your supper, Lian," Mom said. "Don't grill your brother with your questions."

I stuck out my tongue at her. The little girl didn't know a mum can grow from a branch, nor did I care to tell her. I'd wait for a Pining Yellow to bloom in our yard and then break my nifty moneymaking plan to her.

For three days the mum hadn't grown anything, not even a leaf bud. Our hens trod near the twig and then turned away. Dad had once told me a mum emits a scent that tells chickens it's not edible. One night I had a dream that the mum had bloomed overnight—I sold it for ten yuan to Miss Wu who painted me holding my Yellow figurine.

I recalled the dream on Friday morning just before I set off for school, and ran to the yard to check on the twig. As a thick frost covered the ground, the hens hid inside the coop, shivering with cold. All the leaves sagged from the mum's stem. I burst into tears.

I heard Mom holler, "What's the matter with Wei?"

Dad ran out to wrap a coat over my back. "Are you feeling sick, son?" he asked and put his hand on my forehead.

I shook my head. "It's dead . . . dead. . . ."

"What is?"

"The mum I was raising for Miss Wu is dead. I planted the stem in the ground—now it's frozen." I started to cry again.

My older sister had left for school. Mom blocked my younger sister in the doorway. "Go along to school now. Dad will take care of your brother."

"Who is Miss Wu?" Dad asked.

"She's Older Sis's art teacher. She wants the mum to do her painting and win prizes, but it's dead. . . ."

Dad put my arms through my coat sleeves and buttoned the front. "Do you want me to go with you and see her?" He stretched his arm to read his watch. "I have two classes in the morning. Then I can take off."

I muttered, "It's no use now."

"Let me call her to explain the situation," he said. "What

12

business does she have to ask a kid to raise a mum? She's not a biology teacher, obviously. Everybody knows frost season is coming and mums ought to be taken into a greenhouse."

Too upset to say anything, I stood up to return to the house.

"Are you feeling okay now, son?" Mom asked. "Dad will talk to Miss Wu. We must be off to work. Are you ready for school?"

I couldn't think of anything else to do, so I put on my backpack and headed out.

The old man was sticking a bunch of whistles onto the straw mast when I passed by his booth.

"Hey, little brother," he called me. "Have you got a picture of your dog on you?"

"Sure," I mumbled. "I have one in my pencil box."

"So what're you waiting for?" He puffed white breath with every word. "I have a little spare time today. Let me take a look at your dog."

I clutched the straps of my backpack so tightly that I almost stopped breathing. "But I don't have the money."

"Let's check out your dog first, and see if he's as great as you said."

"Of course he is." I threw my backpack on the ground to take out the pencil box. Its plastic cover had become hard with cold, and I tore open a corner as I worked to get Yellow's picture out. I breathed on my hands to warm them.

"He's a stud alright." The man ripped a piece of yellow dough to knead in his palms.

"What're you doing?"

"Just watch."

He pressed his fingers on the dough to make a long muzzle,

and cut a curve at the bottom to give it a grinning mouth. He rolled a pinch of black dough into a ball, sticking a pin twice to bring out the nose! He scraped a piece of white dough, sliced off two round shapes, then put a gray dot in the middle of each to show the hazel eyes. The old man did it all so fast that my eyes felt tired trying to keep up with his fingers. He slid his blade to the side and bent the dough into an ear that hung down from the head, no doubt, of my Yellow!

"Wait." He pushed away my hand to finish the other ear. "Do you see what's missing here?"

"His body."

"You have to pay me to make his body." He jabbed a bamboo stick into Yellow's throat and plugged the head on the top of the mast where I couldn't reach. "He's waiting for you. A cute dog, isn't he? Other kids will like him, too."

I felt dizzy watching Yellow's head hover over me, grinning. The old man touched my hand, and I looked down: it was Yellow's tail! Fuzzy and otter-like, with just the right curve.

"Keep this for me, little brother, so you don't forget about your dog in case I do. What's his name?"

"Yellow."

"A good name for a fine dog."

I wandered off feeling as if my own head had been left on the top of the mast. Then I reached up to pull down my hat and locked my head in place.

I didn't start feeling mad until I was a block away from the candy booth. How could I go to school when Yellow's head was at the stake? He had been eaten once, and couldn't be eaten again by some stupid drooling girl who had eaten Moon Lady.

I had to rescue him this time, even though my parents wouldn't help me and I was on my own.

I needed two and a half yuan, and it was the last day of the mum show. I had to take Pining Yellow before it was too late.

I stamped my foot and sprinted for the park.

Without my sister's help I couldn't climb up the park wall. I waited until a small group of people lined up at the gate, and dashed into the park.

"Hey, you! Where's your ticket?" I heard the voice and started running into the nearest woods. "Come back to the gate!"

The wind cut my face as I kept sprinting. At last, I was out of breath and crashed into a tree. No one was chasing me. The old man must've been the only one on duty today.

There were few tourists, so I spotted Pining Yellow from a distance. Blood rushed into my head and made me so hot that I took off my hat. Entering the garden, I bumped into a park employee who wore a cotton-padded cap with earflaps. He stopped watering the mums and looked me up and down. I began to shiver with cold and decided to leave for a couple of hours, then return at noon when the employees were having their lunch.

I walked onto the lookout pavilion on the lake. The fish were hiding under the thin ice. I dropped stones into the pond trying to scare them out, but they dove deeper into the water where it wasn't frozen. Yellow had caught me a carp in the summer and carried me across the pond and back, so I hadn't learned to swim. I wiped my sole on the mossy deck, knowing that if I slipped into the lake, no one would be there to save me.

The mum show was quiet when I hurried back. The wind

had blown me so numb that the heavy pot almost slipped from my hands as I carried Pining Yellow to the woods. No one saw me. The whole park seemed dead, and I wasn't sure if I was alive. I stumbled until I couldn't walk anymore, and slid down a tree trunk. The sunlight leaking in from the pine needles didn't feel warm on my face. Still, I watched the mum and chuckled.

"Good mum, you're going to the nicest home. Miss Wu really loves you, so you rest assured she'll take care of you." I leaned forward to feel its petals on my cheek. The fishhook tips were soft. "I'm trading you for my Yellow. It's what we both want, isn't it?"

I held the pot between my knees and stroked its leaves, as if they were fur.

At the enclosing wall, I couldn't slide the pot out of a triangle hole on the brick wall. So I dug up Pining Yellow with soil to place it on the wall, its flower pointing inside the park. I stuffed the pot in my backpack. As I left the park, I had a peep at the old man dozing in the gatehouse.

After I found Pining Yellow, I had to rake up more dirt to fill the space left in the pot. My hands felt both warm and cold after the job. I lay on the frosty ground and held up the pot like a trophy, remembering Yellow had been a blind pup when I first got him, and I was starting school.

Miss Wu opened her office door and raised her eyebrows.

"Miss Wu, you said you'd like to buy a species of Pining Yellow, so here it is." I bowed a little to show my sincerity.

"How did you get it?"

"I raised it from a twig that fell on the ground. Like you said, it sprouted and grew and, see, it bloomed!"

"Be honest with me, Wei. Tell me where you got it."

I couldn't think of any way to be honest with her, so I repeated, "I raised it."

"Is it from the park?"

"No."

She crouched down to look me in the eye. "You're too young to be telling lies, Wei. Your dad called to ask me about the twig that you tried to raise."

I began to fear it was a hard sell. She might be tightfisted like my mom. "Aren't you going to buy it?" I stared back at her.

"How much money do you need? I'll give it to you if you return the flower to the park." She held my shoulders. "I might've said something that made you commit the offense, I don't know. If it's your first time, I won't tell your dad. Let's end it here between us."

I struggled free from her grasp. "But I'm selling it to you! I don't want to steal your money."

"Wei, you're stealing from the park."

"They have too many mums and leave them in the wind! Dad said they ought to be kept in the greenhouse today." I wiped my face with my coat sleeve. "You'll take good care of it, won't you? You'll raise more pots and by next month, you can give one to the park." My eyes were suddenly filled with tears. "Somebody stole my Yellow and ate him, before I could have a last look at him. Those thieves were stealing, not me!"

"You, too, if you don't return the mum."

I felt so mad at her that I pounded the office door with my fist, ready to take off. My belly growled, but I was past being hungry. I wanted to give it a last try before letting all my labor be wasted.

"Can I sell it for just two and a half yuan? I have to buy back my Yellow. His head is on a stick at the candy booth."

She watched me with sad eyes as if she were the one who had lost her Yellow. I opened the door and she dragged me back by my arm. "Tell you what, let me buy it for now." She pressed three bills into my palm.

"I'll give you the change on Monday." I dashed for the dough figurine booth, ignoring her calling my name.

I ended up giving Miss Wu her change in the principal's office. My dad paid her back the two and a half yuan and raised my allowance age to eleven. Miss Wu returned Pining Yellow to the park after all, and a park employee called my school. I had to confess about my theft and was put on probation. Dad told the disciplinary committee I hadn't been myself ever since I lost Yellow. They asked me to stay behind to repeat a year's work. If I was as messed up as my dad said, then my theft record might not enter my permanent file.

The good thing was that I got to keep my Yellow figurine, with the nametag that he never had in his life and a super tail that seemed to wag my Yellow. I told the old man I didn't like candy, so he sprayed it with lacquer. It was no longer edible and would last forever. I took a beating at home, but it was nothing, really. Dad kept asking me why I hadn't told him anything. I wondered, what for? He'd only have tried to talk me out of saving Yellow.

⚒—What the Father Wanted . . .

CHIMNEY

held my son facedown on my lap and watched his legs kick in the air like those of a duckling learning to swim. My wife and daughters were pleading for him in chorus, so I had to shout louder.

"How many times have I told you not to cut classes and to do your homework? Tell me, how many times?"

He whimpered and kicked his legs harder. My feet, in hard plastic slippers, began to slide on the cement floor. I took off my right slipper and slapped his butt hard.

My wife grabbed my arm. "Let him go!"

I loosened my grip while my wife pulled him away. She sent our daughters to their rooms to read, and nudged our son to his room to atone for his disgrace: that he would have to repeat the second grade.

I dropped my slipper on the floor, and pinched my temples with my finger and thumb to stop my head from throbbing. After smoking five Lighthouses in half an hour (I had finished off my supply of Peony), I felt the scorching fury in my chest begin to recede.

My wife sat down at the kitchen table and tugged at my elbow. "He's your son," she said. "After all these years, you should know what your own son is like."

"Sometimes I wonder." I heard the grinding of my own teeth and paused. "What did I do in my past life to deserve a son like him?"

"Hush, there's nothing wrong with our son. He's just naughty."

"But there's a line between naughty and wicked."

"He's *not* wicked." My wife stood up.

"Where're you going?"

"To stir-fry a few eggs."

"What for?" I asked. "He's going to stay in the second grade for another year. You're going to reward him with our breakfast eggs? He ought to eat bok choy soup for supper."

"You gave him a good scare," she said.

I could never blame my wife for being so partial to our children that she would give the last egg to our son instead of to me, the head of the household. I knew she was only being logical: the kids were growing, both physically and mentally, while we were merely aging. I was thirty-five, she was thirty-three, our older daughter ten, our son eight, and our younger daughter five. Our son was the thinnest, though he was a vulture at every meal.

My wife laid the golden fried eggs down and sprinkled the dish with a pinch of green onion. Then she took away my cigarette to put it on the ashtray. "Are you cool now?" she asked and held both my hands. "Or do you have to heat yourself up like a chimney and blame it on your son?"

I had first seen her brown freckles after she gave birth to our son Wei. Later, having the younger daughter plumped her up some more. In eleven years of being my devoted wife, she had dodged the one-child policy twice to give me three good-looking children. Her face was still ruddy, but would probably grow sallow in a few years, and her breath was soggy like a mother's. She'd given her very best to the children, and I wondered if she ever saw the futility in it.

I pulled my hands away. "One day he may give me a heart attack."

"It's your own fault if he does. He's just a child, our own son, for goodness sake."

"He sure is." I sighed and stubbed the butt so it didn't burn out. "If he weren't, I wouldn't give a damn about what becomes of his life."

During supper I began to retell the story that I'd told my children half a dozen times.

"I'd been sitting on the unpainted bench outside the delivery room, smoking for hours, careful not to touch or lean on anything. Why? Because it was a hospital, it was where sick people went. Finally, a nurse came out and yelled, 'Hey, are you the husband of the expectant mother?'"

"'Yes, I am.' The girl was impressive in her white coat, so I scrambled up."

"'You have a son.'

"My tense nerves relaxed. I must've grinned so wide that the cigarette fell out of my mouth, and I didn't even notice.

"'Your wife is doing okay.' The nurse grinned, too, showing her little teeth. 'You dropped your cigarette.'

"'Thank you, doctor, thank you so much.' I wanted to shake her hands but didn't—I knew they were sterilized. I was so grateful, so grateful to the little nurse, as if she had bestowed the son upon me! I picked up the cigarette butt and stuck the burning end in my mouth. You see, I was concerned about the nurse's sterilized hands, but I put a dirty cigarette butt into my own mouth! I was beside myself."

My older daughter wiped her mouth with the back of her hand. "Did you burn your lips?" She always worried that people might hurt themselves.

"It was put out when it fell on the floor. The floor was filthy with mud, spit, puke, and who knew what else."

My younger daughter stuck out her tongue loaded with chewed rice. "Did you get ash in your mouth?" She was an imaginative girl.

"A little bit on my tongue, I suppose. I've always told you, 'Diseases enter through the mouth,' so that was a dumb thing to do."

My son picked up a large piece of egg, his fingers sliding down his chopsticks to press it into his mouth. I averted my eyes from the piece of green onion on his nose. I had a queasy stomach that night.

"Listen up, kids. The point of my story is I was very, very happy to have you, son, when you came into this world. So was your mother." I paused when my wife scraped the green onion off our son's nose. "We were overjoyed. There's no earthly reason why you, our only son, have to let us down. We don't ask much from you. Just be a little more gentle and quiet like your sisters. Is that so hard?"

My son kept chewing, his greasy lips half-parted like a piece of red flower. His long-lashed eyes were sweeping over the dishes. There was no sign that he heard me.

My wife reached out to touch his little shoulder. "The one-child policy just came into effect when I was carrying you. I was asked to have an abortion, but I refused. You were so big that I had a difficult labor for nine hours straight. It was a mother's ordeal." She tried to blink away her tears. "You were born beautiful, son. Your sisters were born a little premature, but you were late by almost two weeks. When you were born, you had a full head of black hair, and your bright eyes were already rolling. When the doctor slapped your bottom, your little pecker stiffened. Then you peed on the doctor's white coat! You cried so loud! That was the best moment you ever gave me." She glanced at me, so I took over the lecture.

"The point is, son, we want you to have a little pity on our hearts. One day you'll be a father, too, and you don't want a lawless son, do you?"

I was a little out of it, to say that to an eight-year-old. I hated to beat him, but he made me stone crazy when his school called me every other day. Last semester he had been caught for stealing a pot of chrysanthemum from the park—it got me so angry that I could've had internal bleeding. He'd wasted a year and would be retaught by our upstairs neighbor, whose husband was my department chair. I'd lost face in front of my colleagues and neighbors. They heard about his atrocities at school, then me spanking him at home. Daughters' crying, wife's begging, there wasn't a moment of peace because he lived in this house. Being a father to my son, I had to be the disciplinarian. I'd rather beat him black and blue than have him turn into a juvenile delinquent.

It was already nine-thirty when we finished our supper, two hours behind our regular schedule. The exam papers for my child psychology class were due in the morning. I made a cup of tea for myself and opened a new pack of cigarettes. Then I sat down to grade the papers. After a few exams, I could pick out the scoring and missing points with just a glance, and let the rest of my mind wander off.

Cigarettes helped me relax: I had learned that when I was a lowly university student and sent to the countryside to be reeducated by peasants. I had hoed in the field every day for two years to atone for having bickered against the Cultural Revolution. It was then I took up smoking, the only thing that let me forget about life and its broken promises. With the neat white stick in my fingers, I was a semi-free man, safe with my little indulgence. Many young people in my situation had done worse. There was a lot of casual sex, and various kinds of rapes occurred. I heard of a female student who slept with peasants, then gave birth and dropped the baby directly into a manure pit. I wondered if the umbilical cord had pulled and hurt her at all, when the child was being drowned in the excrement and urine.

I had already lost my bloom (I had it so briefly) when I met a new student, my wife-to-be. My teeth were yellow and black from smoking, and I had become scrawny. I liked her ruddy-cheeked smiles, and we became good friends. The first time I walked with her to the canteen, I told her I had always wanted to become a doctor and save lives with my own hands, but when the college exam time had come, I had to take a color test. I saw only shades of green in the jumbled patterns of color matrix, made some wild guesses, and evidently got them all wrong. Diagnosed as color-blind, I couldn't get into medicine. I took the next closest thing, which was psychology, and chose medicine as my minor. If I had planned to impress her, which I hadn't, I couldn't have done better. She had always been in awe of doctors, though she considered surgery a job of routine violence to cut up sick bodies.

I lingered on the paper at hand, which seemed to be a full hundred marks. I could take a point off its essay question to show him I had a high standard. Instead I put it in the pile with the others. A single hundred wouldn't break the curve, just like a couple of fails didn't make me a bad lecturer. I laid a ninety-mark paper on the top and thought how, compared with medicine, psychology was, after all, more of a theory than a science. Did that ninety-mark student really know less about child psychology than the hundred-mark one? I wouldn't go that far. What did those fresh-faced sophomores know about raising children anyway? Being a psychology professor sure hadn't given me a head start with my son. I had been educated on the Soviet model, and they, too, sent a lot of their scholars to labor camps. Still, I had raised a family to be a haven during the time of turmoil, and it had been, until my son began to grow up.

I finished the last paper, bound the stack, and plucked the rubber band. Then I lit a new cigarette. My wife walked up from behind to wrap her arms around my neck. "Can you not smoke before you come to bed, Chimney?" she asked. "Chimney" was what she called me when the kids weren't around. By then I took it as a term of endearment.

"It relaxes me." I touched her hand. "I've had a long day. Until our son grows up, I can't swear off smoking."

"Come, I want to show you something."

I followed her to our son's room. She slowly opened the side of his quilt and pulled down his little boxers. I saw his black and blue bruises in the shape of my slipper.

I turned away, feeling nauseated. "You know I'm at my wit's end," I said. "I spend more energy on him than I do for both girls, and he's still wayward. How do other parents manage? My three brothers and I, if one of us were half as prankish as Wei, my parents wouldn't have lived to their middle ages."

"Just be patient. He's not like the girls. He's not like other kids." My wife brushed a few stray hairs from his forehead. "All in all, he's our son. Put up with him." She leaned her head on my shoulder.

I nodded. He was an angel in sleep. He was also prettier than the daughters, whose beauty seemed fragile and ephemeral. Even when they were babies, I had watched them and imagined they'd bloom into young women, get married, and then their looks would fade. My son's handsomeness would stick with him to a good age, like his thick skin, his stubbornness. He hadn't begged like my daughters when he was beaten, and he could pig out afterwards as if nothing had happened. Nothing got through to him, which amazed and frustrated me.

My department chair and upstairs neighbor, Wang, was going over the course evaluation forms as I turned in the exam papers.

He shook my hand to tell me, "Looks like you're our star lecturer again."

I won the lecturer's award every year, so this hardly put a smile on my face.

"How was last night?" he asked. So he had heard all the commotion when I spanked my son. "Well, I was just wondering." He put his fist on his mouth to muffle a dry cough.

"My son may have to trouble your wife again next year." I forced a chuckle.

"Not a problem." He passed me a Peony, my favorite cigarette. "I heard he's a bright kid."

I didn't know whether to laugh or curse, being slapped with such a compliment. I almost said, "My son is the biggest challenge of my career," before he lit my Peony. I inhaled with all my might to stop myself from talking about my son.

Wang took out a handkerchief and coughed into it, then wiped his mouth and nose. "My wife asked me to thank you for the hyacinth beans. She loves them, so fresh and crispy."

"Does she really? I'm going to have a harvest. Please stop by whenever you fancy homegrown vegetables. My luffa gourds are plumping up like balloons."

"You know me, I'm a fowl man. A young rooster is my thing. But my wife said she could become a vegetarian with such fresh produce as your hyacinth beans. I thank you for her. Oh." He lowered his voice. "I can get you some Peony ration stamps, if you like."

I burst into a smile. "You're too kind."

Someone walked into the office. Wang patted me on the shoulder and returned to the course evaluation forms.

As I walked down the ramp, I saw my younger daughter standing outside the apartment building. I unlocked the door, and she headed straight to the front yard to check on the hens.

"Three eggs, Dad," she called out from the chicken coop.

I went to the kitchen to put the rice cooker on the stove. "We may get one more this afternoon," I told her. Everyone would be home soon for lunch. It was the kids' last day of school before summer.

"From whom?" She ran inside with two eggs, one in each hand, then turned back for the third.

I studied the brown specks on the eggs she had brought in. "Tomboy," I said. (Tomboy had colorful feathers that were like a rooster's, hence the name.) Nine out of ten times, if not ten, I'd be right.

"Tomboy is going to the delivery crate." She panted. "I can't get the last egg from under her."

"It's all right," I said softly to her uplifted face. My daughters listened to me, but my son didn't. I wondered if a son was deficient in obedience genes. "Would you get me two tender luffa gourds and a shallow basket of hyacinth beans?" I handed her the bamboo basket. "I will cook you gourd egg flower soup and spiced beans."

"Yum." She took it and dashed into the vegetable garden.

My family was allotted the bottom floor because I wasn't a Party cadre but only a professor. It had taken me a while to cultivate the front yard into the admiration of my cadre neighbors. I had built a fine chicken coop and raised eight hens. On top of the cage crawled the luffa gourd and hyacinth bean vines, which grew so heavy last year that they crushed the chicken coop. I had to pick the beans and gourds before they overgrew.

During the harvest season, our family couldn't finish the vegetables and had no fridge to store them, so I gave some away to
Wang, and in turn he gave me Peony ration stamps. Mrs. Wang
had said she envied me for having such a yard. If she could have
one, she'd raise chicks all year long, so Wang wouldn't have to
spend a fortune on young roosters. Of course she was only
flattering me, but still I was pleased to hear it. I loved to hoe in
the fresh air as a break from my mental work. Maybe I had
gotten the habit from two years of working in the fields. Unlike
smoking, it was a good habit I intended to keep.

At the lunch table, I watched my son scoop out the egg flowers
from the serving dish as usual. "Could you be a little more
considerate to others, son? We have five mouths here."

My wife pressed my wrist to calm me. "Dad cooked such
delicious soup, didn't he?" she asked around the table, and both
daughters nodded. My son just looked at me, with his mouth
half open while chewing. "A colleague of mine can get us ten
baby chicks for a bargain. Would you like to take care of them
over the summer, kids?"

The daughters looked at each other and broke into broad
smiles.

"I never raised baby chicks," I said. "It'll be nice to try, and
we have eight hens to look after them, don't we?"

The whole table laughed. Even my son showed his little-
grain teeth. I was cheerful for the first time since last night.

After lunch my wife and I left our older daughter to wash
the dishes, and we went to take a nap. When I woke up half an
hour later, my younger daughter came to me saying, "Dad,
Dad, Tomboy is still laying, is it a difficult labor?"

I wondered where she had learned the term; she had too high an IQ for a girl. My bare feet touched the cement floor before they found my cold slippers. I walked to the chicken coop, opened its door with a squeak, and reached a hand into the wooden crate to feel under Tomboy's fluffy belly. There was only the old egg from this morning. When I nudged her, she pecked me so hard on the hand that it left a pink speck, her eyes fierce. What was wrong with her? I racked my brain for probable causes. Oh, she was broody and would stop laying eggs for a while.

I couldn't have my hens hatch—I needed their eggs for my children. Besides, none of their eggs was fertilized. There hadn't been a rooster down here. Tomboy had been the star egg layer for weeks; no wonder she was coming down with a hormone imbalance. I had to cure her. As I had once learned from working on the farm, birth control pills might work. My wife could get them at the drugstore for free, a side benefit of the one-child policy. She was already up and dressed. I told her about Tomboy's condition. She agreed to get me the pills that afternoon.

My wife told the three children before they were off to school, "The baby chicks will be home waiting for you all."

My son came home early at four-thirty, a record during the last two months. He sprinted toward us yelling, "Baby chicks!"

They were the cutest lemon furballs, waddling in the rattan basket and chirping in panic as if calling their mom. My wife said, "Be gentle!" as my son grabbed a screeching chick.

"Be good, be good now, that's a dear." He stroked its little head and made it totter in his palm.

I wished he had arrived a little later. I took Tomboy to the far end of the coop and pried open her beak. She screamed as if I were killing her!

"What're you doing, Dad?" my son asked.

"Uh, it's just—Tomboy needs a little medicine." I turned my back on them.

"Tomboy was having a difficult labor today, so Dad is curing her," my younger daughter said. I heard my wife's laugh.

"Really, Dad?" my son shouted.

"Sort of." I stuffed the round white pill in her beak, but she coughed it back out. My son stepped over and watched us curiously. "Do you mind breaking the pill into two pieces, son? It's too big for her throat." He tried to break the pill but it was slippery, so he started to put it into his mouth and bite it. "NO!" I yelled, relieved to see him drop the pill in a shudder. "The pill was spat out, it's dirty." I wouldn't mention birth control. "It's okay if you can't do it. Call Mom."

"No, I can." He scratched on the line in the middle of the pill with his thumbnail. Then he broke it into two and gave me the large piece.

I put it at the root of Tomboy's tongue and then pressed her beak shut. The hen's eyes opened and closed for a few times as if she'd vomit. I waited until her eyes returned to normal, opened the beak and saw the pill had gone down, took the smaller piece from my son and fed it to her as well. Then I stroked the hen's neck and released her. She flew across the yard and bounced back from the picket fence, crowing as though she were mad. Poor Tomboy, be good or you are sure to suffer.

"Dad, what did you give Tomboy?" my son asked, as we walked back to the porch.

"It's a prescription." I couldn't lie to my little helper. "The pill helps balance hormones, so Tomboy will lay eggs instead of wasting her time hatching." I patted his small back. "Thank you, son."

"Sure." He ran to play with the chicks.

I fed my hens cooked chaff mixed with chopped pig entrails, high fiber and high protein. This was too hard for baby chicks to digest, and their beaks were too tiny to pick up long-grain rice, so the next day I decided to go out and buy bird food. My older daughter could babysit for a couple of hours. I told her to ask Mrs. Wang upstairs for help if anything should arise.

Then I went to visit Mrs. Wang with four luffa gourds and a full basket of hyacinth beans. I asked her to look after the children while I was away.

"Sure thing." She ushered me inside with a broad grin on her face. "Will you be gone for long?"

"Just a couple of hours. I need to buy some grains for the baby chicks."

"Is that what you heard last night?" she asked Lily, her seven-year-old daughter, who came to sit by me on the sofa. "How fine to raise chickens in such a yard! Old Wang talked to me about raising chicks on our little balcony. Can you believe it? I said sure, if you'd swear off cigarettes, and that settled it. Oh, he has some ration stamps for you."

After she stepped out, Lily grabbed my arm and kneeled on the sofa to whisper in my ear, "Can I go play with the chicks, Uncle? I saw them last night, so cute. Mom didn't let me come down. She said Wei was in trouble."

I avoided her round eyes. But really, my son wasn't a secret.

I had spanked him for hitting Lily before. "Okay, if you don't mind Wei," I told her.

"Here're a few ration stamps for this month." Mrs. Wang entered, while Lily dashed out shouting, "Ma, I'm going out to play."

"Okay Lily, don't go far," she said and turned toward me. "You rest assured that I'll look after the kids."

I thanked her and left.

Wang was a heavier smoker than I was. Lately he'd been coughing and having chest pain, so he decided to cut back. As the college admission time was near, every once in a while, some parents, carrying cartons of Kent or Marlboro, knocked on my door to ask where Director Wang lived. Wang must've grown tired of Peony, China's best cigarettes, so he gave me the ration stamps because I was his friend. That was one of the few benefits of having a cadre neighbor. It was only the second week of June, but I felt like buying the cigarettes that day since I was out shopping alone and spared my wife's nagging.

It took me nearly three hours to get the Peony and then the grains. (I didn't want to carry the heavy grain bag to line up for cigarettes, so I ended up waiting in two very long lines.) I rode home on my bike, with the precious grocery bag hanging down from the handlebars and the bag of grains clamped on the backseat, feeling elated about my windfall of Peony.

The door was not locked, so I pushed my bike inside and ground over one of my hard plastic slippers. I took my bag of Peony to hide in the armoire. The three children, pressing together at the end of the sofa, gaped at me when I walked in.

"Did you have fun while I was away?" I joked and closed the

armoire door. Then I caught sight of my son's face, grayish with tears and mucus marks. He was biting on his thumbnail as if trying not to cry. "What happened?" I was startled to hear my own voice.

"Wei killed a chick," my younger daughter said.

"How?" I held my breath and clenched my fists.

"He wore your slippers and stepped on it," my older daughter replied.

I inhaled, held my breath, exhaled, and relaxed my fists. For a minute I didn't know what to say. My son's bare feet were only half of my shoe size. He must've been dragging those slippers like a waddling goose. Luckily I hadn't been home to hear it. I touched his shoulder and felt him wince under my hand.

"Tell me what happened." I heard a tremor in my voice and cleared my throat.

He crouched down a bit to stare at his bare feet.

"I won't get angry. If it's dead, it's dead. Just tell me what happened." I drew out one word at a time as if from a deep well inside my chest.

He began with a nasal sound. "Lily was chasing me, so I ran out to the porch. I jumped into the yard and felt something soft, like mud. Lily stopped. I looked behind me, the chick was lying flat on its side. Then it tried to get up, like it was going to be okay, but it sprang to the fence, then bounced back. When it did it again, blood sprayed out of its neck. It jumped a few more times, spraying blood, then it lay still in the field." He began to sob.

I heard the door open. My wife was back. She came in and asked, "What's going on?"

My son was still sobbing. I ran my hands down his arms and

held his shaky body. "You have no business to wear my slippers, and you should've watched where you were going." I explained to my wife, "He killed a chick, wearing my slippers, but it was an accident. I won't scold you. We'll bury it later, okay?" He sniffed a long strand of mucus back into his nostril, and I released him.

My wife sat dumbly for a minute, looking at me, then at him and our daughters, before she took him to the bathroom to wash his face. I found my right slipper lying in the yard beside the dead chick, and pinched it up with two fingers. When the bathroom was free, I went in to scour both of my slippers with soap and a luffa sponge and wiped them dry on the towel. Dropping one on the floor, I held the right slipper to my nose. It smelled not of blood but lightly of soap, so I rinsed it again and washed my hands, then took off my shoes and socks to put on the slippers.

My son kept a crying face at dinner. It was so odd to see him shocked like this that it almost made me smile. After dinner I went to the porch and smoked my Peony, while the light shone on the dead chick in the field. Pity if it was a little hen, she could've laid eggs in a few months. Oh well. If my stubborn son learned a lesson, it would be well worth it.

While I was having my third cigarette, my son came to me and whispered, "Dad."

"Are you ready?" I stubbed out the butt.

He stole a glance at the field. "Yes."

"Take your shovel. We'll bury it under the luffa gourd. Do you want me to carry it over?"

"No, I will."

He stood on the lowest step and reached down to pick up the little chick by a thin leg. His face turned white. He ran to my side and dropped it on the ground, clutching my leg, his dirty hands rubbing on my ivory pants. I waited until he loosened his grip, squatted down and dug a few spadefuls into the ground.

"Now do you want to finish it?" I asked him.

He nodded and began to dig with his little shovel, splashing dirt onto my pants and slippers. I didn't move. My wife and daughters were watching us from the porch.

"Can I put it in now?" he asked in a whiny voice.

"You decide for yourself," I told him, "young man."

He measured the chick's body with his hand and dug a few more times. "Is it okay now?"

"Yes," I said softly.

He picked up the chick by its foot and dropped it into the hole with a shiver. Then he began to scoop, and I stopped him. "Look at it for a minute, say you're sorry, and you'll be more careful with things in the future."

"I'm sorry."

His features were convulsed so I told him, "Now you can bury her."

He shoveled so fast that he had to stop twice to catch his breath. I just watched him. The porch light on the upstairs balcony was turned on, then off.

My younger daughter asked, "Do you guys need help?"

"No." He wiped his forehead. "I got it."

He flattened the mound with the back of his shovel. Then he crouched down as if he'd throw up. He sprang up and dashed for the porch, and I followed him. My wife reached out to touch him, but he veered straight to his room. He went to bed early that night.

Throughout the summer my son pulled a few tricks that made me want to shout and laugh at the same time. After I made rice wine, he fed some to the chicks and made them all drunk, lying in the field as if they were dead. Another day he played with Lily, and Mrs. Wang gave him a small goldfish as a gift. He kept it in a bowl for two days, and then practiced fishing for it when it looked like it was dying. The hens, under my care, kept laying eggs. But they didn't like the chicks at all, and pecked them viciously whenever they dared to eat from the hens' pot. We lost a few more chicks to natural diseases. When the fall came, we had only three young hens and a rooster to join the chickens.

Just before school started, the faculty had routine health checkups. Wang was diagnosed with stage 2 lung cancer. He wasn't even forty years old, with a fourteen-year-old son crippled from polio and Lily. It was such a catastrophe and, worst of all, unexpected and undeserved. For two weeks all sorts of people came to console the family with fruits and tonics. Then his life quieted down as if he were waiting to die. Meanwhile, our rooster began to crow at four o'clock in the morning and woke up the whole neighborhood. We needed to get rid of it, so I took it to Wang, but he refused and joked it was probably time for him to become a vegetarian. I realized he didn't want to stain his own hands with a rooster's blood at a time like this.

I proposed to my family that we kill the rooster and cook it for Wang.

Before I could finish my reasoning, my son interrupted me. "It's mine. I raised the rooster. You can't just butcher it."

"We all appreciate it, son. But we really can't have a rooster in the neighborhood." Besides the crowing at dawn, there were neighbors' hens to be considered, but I didn't have to tell him that.

"Would you like us to sell it at the farmers' market?" my wife asked.

"No."

"Would you rather eat it yourself?" I asked him.

"No!" he said. "Dad, you fixed Tomboy once. Can you do that for the rooster?"

I was struck dumb, and my wife laughed loudly. "No, son, it only works on hens." I waited for him to grill me, but he didn't. Or maybe he knew. He was a bright kid.

"I guess we'll have to let the Wangs have it, then. I hope it'll do some good."

He sounded so generous that I gazed at him with awe. He had grown three centimeters in the summer, and his little tummy had diminished. Soon his voice would begin to change, and he would grow a furry moustache. I shook my head, *no, not so fast*. He was only nine years old.

After giving the rooster stew to the Wangs, Wei returned downstairs with my wife.

"Lily was almost crying," he said.

Smoking a Peony, I tried in vain to forget about Wang's impending death. "You see how poor Lily is, now that her father's days are numbered." I felt tight in my throat. "You kids should feel lucky that we're young, strong, and by your side."

My son said, "Mrs. Wang told us lung cancer is caused by smoking. Dad, aren't you in danger too?"

I flicked an ash stick off my Peony. "That is *not* my point." After a pause I added, "You kids should leave the parents alone."

"Why?"

I couldn't think of a good reason. "There're many things you don't know." I looked to my wife for help, but she turned her face away.

"Mom promised Mrs. Wang that she'd make you quit smoking." He pulled her hand and watched her face. "Didn't you, Mom?"

She squeezed his shoulder. "We'll talk about that later, Wei."

He stood before me and plucked the cigarette from between my lips. "Dad, will you quit?"

That was too much. I didn't need that, *not* that. I'd been in such grief for Wang that I didn't want to go upstairs. I might've broken down in tears if he had rejected our rooster stew.

My wife said, "Don't get rude with your dad," but she was smiling.

My daughters stared wide-eyed at my face.

I snatched the cigarette from his hand. "Where were you when I took up smoking?" I pointed my cigarette butt at his face. "Son, you peed on the doctor's coat when I dropped my cigarette outside the delivery room. Who gave you the right to tell *me* what to do?"

"If I try to be good, Dad, will you quit?"

The cigarette fell from my fingers. I stooped to pick up the butt from the cement floor but didn't want to put it back into my mouth. My chest tightened with anger, though I knew I mustn't get mad. What if, what if he meant the challenge? It'd be a bargain—well, not for me, but it'd be a bargain for the family, and the sort of bargain that I'd been waiting for since he was born. What more could I ask from my naughty son, if he would make an effort to grow up, for my sake?

"If I quit, will you behave?" I stuttered.

"I will try, of course." His eyes were clear and brave. "I won't try unless you swear off cigarettes."

I stubbed out the butt and stood up to open the armoire door. "Will you bring me a garbage bag, son?" My wife nudged him toward the kitchen. I dumped the carton of Lighthouse into the bag that my son held and dusted my hands. "There you have it, son. From now on you have to behave."

He reached his hand into the drawer. "You're not done yet!"

"Excuse me." I grabbed his arm and took out the open carton of Peony. As I reached for the last pack, I pulled out a cigarette to slide it under a stack of paper, then dropped the pack into his bag as well. I was entitled to have a last Peony, after what I had sacrificed. "All right?" I asked him. "Are we happy now? I'm throwing away Peonies, too, for your sake."

He put out his pinkie. "Deal."

We hooked fingers and made a solemn pact. My wife and daughters were our witnesses. I felt both ludicrous and completely sincere. From now on, if one of us broke his vow, we both would be shamed, like father, like son.

Come to think of it, my son might be more gifted in psychology than I was, and he wasn't even color-blind.

母—What the Mother Did Not Know . . .

THE BIRTHDAY GIRLS

I knelt on the plush mat before the image of Guanyin, and decided not to prostrate myself on the ground like peasant women who prayed for begetting sons. Peering up at Guanyin's white-hooded statue, I marveled at her virginal beauty. Her slender figure was seated on the white lotus throne with one knee raised so that her little slipper peeped from beneath her robe. She held her willow sprig in the vase of the sweet dew, ready to sprinkle the nectar of compassion upon every head equally. On either side of her stood her attendants: Shancai, a smiling boy, and Longnü, the Dragon Maiden who cupped a giant red pearl in both her hands.

My younger daughter crouched down beside me to whisper, "You're superstitious, Mom."

I muttered, "Hail to Guan Shi Yin Bodhisattva," twice and gripped my daughter's shoulder to stand up. "Don't be a simpleton," I said. Then I wondered if it was harsh to call my twelve-year-old—no, two weeks to twelve—names.

Locking arms, we strolled to the back of the shrine. I breathed in the incensed air, my eyes feasting on the colorful plaster statues in the dim temple light.

My daughter said, "School taught us there aren't fairies or spirits, ghosts or gods. Guanyin, the so-called goddess of mercy and giver of offspring, is folk, not fact."

"Hush." I stooped down and rubbed my cheek against hers, so that she'd look up with me at the Guanyin statue towering above the layers of clouds on the wall. I didn't want to point because it would be irreverent. "Isn't she magnificent?"

The thousand-eyed, thousand-armed Guanyin wore her suit of armor like a handsome prince, with golden arms fanning out behind her back like sunrays, like weaponry. Each arm had a unique gesture with its elbow and hand, which showed an open eye inside each palm. There was nothing more regal in the temple, not even Amitābha Buddha himself.

"Mom, it's just a statue."

"Listen," I said. "You were born on Guanyin's birthday, the Hearer of Cries. Guanyin relieves the suffering of all who call out her name, whether deserving or not."

My daughter pulled away and ran outside. I bowed hastily and followed, squinting and covering my eyes from the bright sunlight. My daughter leaned on the banister with her feet squished inside the column dividers. Red carp swam in the pool among pink lotus flowers. The bell of the temple sounded in the courtyard.

"Hail to Guan Shi Yin Bodhisattva," I prayed.

My daughter groaned and let go of the railing. I caught her by the waist and tugged her down from the banister. She wiggled until her feet touched the ground.

"Mommy, I want Nikes because they're the coolest thing in school."

"You can be better than cool." I kneaded the side of her cheek. It was a new mole, not dirt. "Daughter, you can be blessed."

She grinned wide to show me her crowded front teeth. "See what I mean? Mom, you're superstitious."

"Humph! What does a little girl know?

"To the frogs in a temple pool
The lotus stems are tall;
To the Gods of Mount Everest
An elephant is small.

"Now let's find Dad, your brother, and sister and go for a row."

My younger daughter talked back to me just like a Fire Dragon. The year of her birth, 1976, had too much yang aspect and not enough yin for a girl. Her element is wood, and since wood feeds fire, she is quite a feisty girl for her yin-ridden Ox mother. Yet Dragon is the sign of royal power, so I had been overjoyed to find myself pregnant, even though the one-child policy was promoted then and she would've been our third. The woman cadre in my work unit had pressed me to have an abortion. I am an Earth Ox, you see, not a pushover for such tactics, so I waited for it to blow over to have my Dragon son. Oh, yes, I wanted a son; what mother can resist the idea of having a Dragon boy who will brave the world and succeed?

I poured out my prayers to Guanyin and dragged my whole family to the temple to burn joss sticks before the graffiti-defaced image of the goddess. In 1976, the temple was still a ruin after the Cultural Revolution, so we could have a picnic in the courtyard that was running to weeds. There on the grass, watching my five-year-old girl and three-year-old boy gobble down their boiled eggs, I listened to crickets chirping and felt the new life move in my belly like pure joy. It was as if I had borne my first two children for my husband to carry on his family line, and saved the third for my own. For the first time, it felt like mine, *all* mine.

That night I dreamt I would have a male heir, who would invite me one day to visit his home in a helicopter. "Why a chopper, not a jet?" I asked the Dragon Maiden who brought me the news.

She scoffed, "Humph!" and vanished.

The next day I stood on the porch step and racked my brain about the riddle, while our upstairs neighbor's laundry dripped onto my head. A chopper can land almost anywhere, even on the roof of a mansion, which implied my "son" would grow to possess such affluence I could only dream of.

Then, on July fifteenth, a drizzling Thursday, I slipped on the mossy deck by the well and was hurried into labor. After five hours of screaming pain, I felt like I had been cheated out of my deal when I found a slit instead of a pecker on my beautiful baby. She came two weeks early on the nineteenth of the sixth lunar month at 3:16 in the afternoon. I changed "his" name from *Lian*, as in integrity, to *Lian*, as in lotus flower, which meant spotless purity arising from fetid mud. Born before 1982, when the one-child policy was enforced with financial penalty, Lian, my heir, was both a blessing and a bargain.

Our children hopped onto the rented rowboat and grabbed their oars. Lian sat across from our two older children, so my husband took her side while I did the other. I felt the body weight on board was unevenly distributed, but Lian was grinning behind her oar so I let her have her way. My husband pushed his oar against the shore, and our boat left port amidst the kids' cheering.

I saw a silver carp glide by and pulled up my oar. "Kids," I said. "Try not to disturb the fish too much. To them we're just tourists, you know."

My younger daughter tittered beside me. She struck her oar so deeply in the water that her little body shook with effort and her tongue stuck out as she rowed.

"Take it easy, Lian," my husband said. "You're making the boat spin."

"But we're rowing against the three of them," Lian said.

"It's not a race, Lian," her father said. "We're having fun."

"Exactly," I said. "So are the fish in the lake." Lian slowed down, while I backed my oar a couple of times to keep our boat heading straight.

"We had fun in the Guanyin Temple, didn't we?" I asked Lian, who stared wide-eyed at me. "This is the Earth Dragon year, an auspicious time for you, daughter."

She grinned from ear to ear. "You mean I'll get my Nikes?"

I wrinkled my nose to make a frown. "Why Nikes? They're bulky and ugly."

"Excuse me, Mom?" my older daughter said. "Expensive things are not all ugly."

"Especially imported goods," my son added.

It was annoying to have your own children turn on you, so I tried to back off. "Lian, I'd be happy to buy you the Nikes, if your feet weren't growing like crazy." I reached over to press her toes in the opening of her sandal. "You just got these in the spring, and see how tight they've grown. Maybe you should get a pair of sandals instead, if you want to be cool."

She bit her lips and pulled the wet oar onto her lap. "If I buy a larger pair of Nikes, they may last for six months."

"Then what'll we do—throw them away? Don't forget three hundred yuan is Mom's monthly salary." I jabbed at the knee of my husband. He was supposed to back me up. "We should spend it on a gift that counts," I prompted him.

"Crossing the bridge opening, sailors!" He pushed his oar against the pier so hard that I wavered to grab the side of our boat.

"Don't scare me like that, old man! I was talking business to Lian!"

"So was I." He scooped an oarload of lake water and splashed it over me and Lian. We screamed and stared at each other in drenched clothes. I tried to catch my breath because I was laughing so hard. Lian smacked her oar on the water while her dad protested, "Hold on a sec, let me close the camera lens!"

After our boat pulled into shore, the two girls and I dashed into the ladies' room. I wiped my wet blouse with sheets of paper, then opened my folding fan. My older daughter joined me, and we giggled. Then I heard my younger daughter's voice in the stall.

46

"Oh, hell."

We turned our faces to listen. "What's the matter, baby?" I asked.

"My pad is messed up. Yuck."

My older daughter made a face then ran outside.

"Do you want me to help you?" I asked.

"I've got a clean pad, but my panties are wet." She emerged from the stall with her face flushed. "Periods are disgusting."

She washed her hands and dried them on the side of her cotton skirt, ignoring the handkerchief balled in her pocket. She saw me watching and stuck out her tongue. I felt like prodding my thick-skinned daughter.

"Remember what you said four months ago?" I pulled her close to fan her wet skirt.

"About what?"

"About how you would never have that 'thing' Mom had, you know?" She had boasted when seeing me wash my stained underwear that she would be neat and clean like her dad.

She tilted her head to recall those words. Then her cheeks turned bright red. She looked me in the eye unflinchingly as her skirt puffed up under my fan.

I pinched her cheek gently. "See how soon your 'never' went?"

She tossed her head to be free of me and ran outside. I fanned my wet shirt a few more times but became impatient with my fastidiousness. Who would notice me, a thirty-nine-year-old mother, wearing a padded bra inside her half-dry blouse? My blooming daughters made no fuss about their looks. I slammed my fan shut and hurried out to join them.

A week later I dropped by the athletic shoe store on my way home. Its hip, brown-colored glass-front seemed hostile. Next door was a jewelry store with a sign "60% off liquidation." I squeezed my handbag under my arm and veered into the jewelry store instead.

Almost two hours later, I headed home with a pair of Nikes. I wished I had gotten the pendant of Guanyin instead, the piece of deep green jade engraved with the divine image. It would grow greener after being worn close to the skin. Body heat warms up jade; I knew that because my mom had once given me a pendant. So that I could be there with her in the afterlife, I had it buried with her when she passed away from breast cancer. Lian had never met her grandmother, whose name I had cried out in pain while giving birth to my children. When I had first taken Lian into my arms, I had been more hurt than disappointed, knowing my heir was fated to grow up and have this great birth pang, that her being a Dragon made no difference.

I got home and flashed the Nike box at Lian. I didn't feel like keeping a secret tonight.

"Three hundred yuan!" she screeched when she saw the receipt inside.

I was touched. We weren't used to buying the children gifts. But the twelfth year is special because one's own zodiac sign returns and it begins a new cycle. Lian looked lovely with her round chin and slim shoulders. I wondered how the jade pendant would have hung on her chest.

"You're a lucky girl," I said, "to be born perfect on Guanyin's birthday."

"Whatever." She ran to show her dad the gift.

Because I had been missing my mom and caring for my daughters, I couldn't bear her "whatever" tonight. Following her to the kitchen, I raised my voice. "It's not 'whatever,' daughter. You think your birthday is yours, yours alone. Well, you're wrong. It belongs to me as well, the mother who brought you here."

"Watch out, ladies, hot stew coming through." My husband carried the clay pot cooker to the dinner table. "What's going on?"

"Our daughter thinks her birthday has nothing to do with me."

"That's not what I meant," Lian said.

"I know you didn't mean anything," I said. "You never mean anything. What do you care? Except for getting your shoes."

"Am I missing something here?" My husband fumbled in the Nike box. "Lian's birthday is not tonight, is it? Good, let's feed first, and worry about business later. Come on now, both of you, sit, it's late. Dinner time, boy and girls."

Lian took her seat at the table obediently as I grabbed the Nike box to hide it inside the highest drawer in our armoire.

After dinner, I left the children home studying and nudged my husband outside to take a stroll in the fields. The full moon hung in the sky like a golden plate amidst the glittering stars. Being alone with my husband of eighteen years, I felt like a young woman again.

"Husband, do you think we're raising good children?"

"No doubt. Why do you ask?"

"Sometimes I wonder if I'm too crazy about them for my own good. They're just kids, you know. What'll happen when they grow up?"

"They'll be grateful to their mother."

"I'm not so sure."

We walked arm in arm on the gravel ridge.

"Is something bothering you, Wife?"

"To be honest, I don't feel good buying Lian a pair of sneakers she won't wear for more than a couple of months." We strolled a few steps in silence. "I want to give her something more lasting and precious. Guess what I found today."

"Go ahead and tell me."

"A jade Guanyin pendant with the finest glow. But we can't afford to buy her two gifts. Besides, we have to be fair to our three kids."

"How much is the pendant?"

"Two hundred and fifty yuan, with 60 percent off because the store was in liquidation. I'd rather have bought her a pair of sneakers made in China for fifty yuan than thrown away three hundred on some imported footwear. How good is that?"

"I see." He wrapped his arm around my waist.

I struggled out of his embrace. "Husband, I have to ask you something." I avoided his twinkling eyes. "Be serious. Do you think I'm superstitious?"

"Except for the few times when you went overboard, you're a fine mother."

I threw my arms around his neck. "It's good to hear *you* say that. If I hadn't met you, old man, I might've shaved my head and gone to a nunnery."

He hugged me tightly against his chest. "Thank Guanyin that I crossed your path."

We beamed at each other and resumed walking. "When you think about it, what's so good about being a mother? You give your children whatever you can scrape together, while they just take, take, and laugh at your good intentions. In a nunnery, you can at least work on your own salvation."

"Are you talking about the pendant again?"

I spun around to face him. "Hail to Guan Shi Yin Bodhisattva! I want Lian to have the amulet." I took a deep breath. "That's it. I feel better already."

"Done," he said.

"What?"

"Your wish is granted, Wife. Guanyin has heard your prayer."

I thought of my chopper dream and giggled. Sure, I was crazy about Lian, but what was the harm in believing? Like an indulgent parent, Guanyin is kind and will grant one any wish so long as it is not evil.

I woke up early on August 1, the nineteenth day of the sixth lunar month. The sky was a hot white, cicadas screaming outside my windows. Feeling a dull throb in my head, I tried to brace up for a hectic Monday.

I left work an hour early to buy grilled meats, pot-stewed fowl, and cupcakes, along with joss sticks, which were cheaper in the grocery store than at the temple. The thought of swinging by the jewelry store flashed through my mind as I biked home, but I dismissed the idea. It was Lian's big day.

After the feast, I took out the plastic bag that contained the shoebox, eyeing the grin on Lian's face. "Here is our gift to you for being our precious daughter."

"Will you open it for me, Mom?" She cupped her cheeks in her hands. "I'm totally psyched."

I reached into the bag and felt the canvas uppers of sneakers bound by their laces. The label read, "Shanghai Soaring Sneakers."

"What happened to the Nikes?" I gasped and dumped out the bag. I heard a click on the floor, and picked up a piece of green jade tied to a red satin ribbon. It had the divine glow of the Guanyin statue.

"Happy birthday to you, too, Mommy!" the children cheered.

When they sang me the birthday song, I wished I could've disappeared into a hole in the ground. "Nonsense. Who returned the Nikes?" My voice cracked like a sob in a laugh.

My husband patted Lian's head. "You underestimated our Dragon maiden."

"Wait, we're not done yet," Lian said. "Mom, each of us has a birthday gift. You can choose either the sneakers or the pendant. Keep in mind that we can exchange the shoes for a pair in your size, but we have to keep the pendant because the store doesn't give refunds. What do you say?"

I cupped the jade in my palm. Guanyin holds one hand close to the heart, and the other lightly upon the knee to form the gesture of bestowing gifts. Her round cheeks and chin blurred into Lian's face before my wet eyes. "Lian, you need the shoes more than I do. The thing about jade is, I can warm it up for you. You take it when you leave home, so I'll be with you wherever you go." I opened my palm to show her the image of goddess and asked, "Who else's birthday is today?"

"Guanyin, the Hearer of Cries," Lian replied with pride on her tender face.

"Let me get you ready for the rite." I crouched down to slide her feet into the sneakers and tie up the laces.

Lian walked around and stooped to press her toes. "Mom, they'll last me for six months."

She showed me the grin that melted my heart like a marshmallow in a hearth. How could I help myself? Everything I did, I did for her.

When we arrived at the temple for the evening rite, the Guanyin shrine was ablaze with candles and incense. I held Lian's hand tightly in mine, as if she might grow wings and fly away. I knew a real Dragon has strong karma and can take shape of other creatures; a chopper or a jet is of no consequence.

"Lian, I want to tell you about the birth of Guanyin." I felt the warmth of a blush spread across my face. "You may call it a fable, but it doesn't matter." I raised my eyes to the thousand-eyed, thousand-armed Guanyin statue. "The male deity Guanyin crossed over from India to China and became a goddess who assumes thirty-three appearances to help people in need, seven of which are female: a nun, a Buddhist laywoman, a woman, a housewife, an officer's wife, a Brahman woman, and a lovely young girl."

Lian leaned against my side. "Wow."

"Not 'wow.'" I brushed her stray hair to the back of her ears. "Just call out her name, and merciful Guanyin will grant your wish." I stooped to whisper into her ear, "It works."

She blinked. "Does Guanyin really have a thousand eyes and arms?"

"Count for yourself." I took her soft hand in mine to point at the emblems, one by one. "That open hand with fingers points downwards, and the sweet dew pours from the eye in the palm to assuage hunger and thirst.

"A long-life vase signifies all that is virtuous and loving.

"A white lotus signifies the attainment of merit.

"A precious mirror signifies wisdom.

"A bow signifies a glorious career.

"A precious volume signifies achieving great learning."

Then a sweet note was struck, and to the throb of the wooden fish drum a chant rose:

> "True Guanyin! Pure Guanyin!
> Immeasurably wise Guanyin!
> Merciful and filled with pity,
> Ever longed-for and revered!"

When another note struck upon an angle iron, monks and nuns slipped from their places to form a single file that wound its way about the temple hall, circling the altar and statues behind it. The patter of cloth-soled feet quickened to a run, while the chant shortened to an urgent "Hail to Guan Shi Yin Bodhisattva." Then came a deep chime and the coiled line diminished, one by one, into silence.

To my last day, I'll remember the creek of bamboo swaying in the wind, the tender-hearted Guanyin with her right hand raised in benediction, her elongated eyes half closed in contemplative bliss. The stumps of votive candles guttered at her feet, and the stubs of the incense sticks lit in her honor perfumed the air.

"Hail to Guan Shi Yin Bodhisattva!" Lian said with her palms pressed together.

"Happy birthday to us all," I prayed.

THE WILLFUL TEENAGERS

子—With Whom the Son Took Liberties . . .

IF YOU WERE MY LEGEND

had been trying to kick my sister Lian out of my room but to no avail. Having caught me listening to music while doing my homework, she insisted that I owed her at least a half-hour with me in my room, or she would tell my parents.

I knocked my elbows against my desk repeatedly to make a rhythmic noise, while she read *The Little Mermaid* lying in my bed. Twelve years old and she still read comic books. I was three years older but felt as if I were an uncle stuck with a bratty niece. My older sister had become busy with college prep courses, so we rarely saw her in the house. Mom told me how lucky I was to have gotten a little sister before China's one-child policy took effect, but I only saw my misfortune. I picked up my watch and wound it forward.

"Time's up." I poked her ankle. "Get out."

She tossed her head to make her bangs slide across her forehead. "Has time gone by so fast? Oh my!" she exclaimed in a flirtatious tone that didn't become her at all.

I slapped my wrist with my watchband. "Another minute passed—scram!"

She got off my bed, walked to my stereo, and pressed the eject key. I grabbed her wrist and, with my free hand, pushed the cassette player closed. She thrust her hand forward, reaching for the eject key.

"I want to see what you were listening to!" she screeched.

"Mind your own business." I shoved her outside, then bolted my door. The tape I had listened to was Zhou Yan's album *If You Were My Legend,* my treasured possession. I would have sooner thrown it away than let Lian lay her paws on it.

My contempt for Lian was matched only by my love for Zhou, who had been my classmate and best friend for three years. Tomorrow Zhou would finish her concert tour and return to Nanjing, when I would declare my love to her. The rest of my summer would be a happy one if she would be my girlfriend.

I switched on the pendant lamp by the side of the mosquito net, then lifted the bamboo mat to expose the poster of Zhou spread on my bedframe. The picture was wrinkled with the line marks of the mat and the crisscrosses of the strung coir ropes of my bed frame. The pale yellow light cast a magnified halo over her oval face, her neck, and the plateaus below her perfect collarbones.

I heard Mom's footsteps, flipped my bamboo mat back down, and quietly unbolted my door. Just before the door opened, I crawled into the mosquito net and lay down. Mom's hand tucked the net and poked my shoulder.

"'Night, son." She switched off the light.

"'Night, Mom."

I turned slowly to lie on my stomach, pressing my crotch against the fine grids of the bamboo mat. My friend Qu said young guys like us should sleep with girlfriends so they could love us more. I had taken to sleeping with the poster, my substitute for Zhou while I couldn't be with her in person.

Already I felt a warm tingling between my legs. Sometimes I woke up in the middle of night with gooey underpants and lingered in the glorious pleasure my dream about Zhou had brought me. Qu had told me to never doubt that I could win Zhou's love; otherwise, she would see right through my diffidence and laugh at me for being weak. But I trusted Zhou too much to believe she would turn me away disappointed. After I had endured a long torturous summer, shadowed by my sister, I couldn't lose heart on this last night before her return.

I woke to a pounding on my door. "Brother, can I borrow your drawing compasses?"

I pressed the pillow against my ear to shut out her shrill voice. She pushed open my door and stomped inside. I heard the marbles roll in my desk drawer as she pulled it out. She fumbled for something, then slammed the drawer closed.

"Get out," I told her.

She punched my mosquito net on her way out.

The gauze net trembled around me like it was about to collapse and throw a shroud upon me. I should've persuaded my parents to send Lian to a summer camp, but they wanted to save money. Had I not been counting down the days to Zhou's return, I would've been so fed up with Lian that she would not have dared to enter my room without my permission.

Now that I was worked up about Lian, it was no use to try to sleep anymore. I sat up on my bamboo mat and sneezed loudly. Last summer I hadn't had an allergy to pollens. Qu said it was one of the sure signs that I was becoming a grown man. I let out another loud sneeze and rubbed my sore nose. The bed frame thumped with my weight, as I propped my hands on its edge to hop onto the floor.

Dad stopped me at the bathroom door. "Son." He pointed between my legs. "Put on a pair of pants, will you?"

I looked down and saw a bulge in my boxers, which pumped like a raised sail. "What's wrong?" I asked myself as well as him.

"You can't walk around the house like this," he said. "What's been on your mind lately?"

"Nothing."

I covered the front of my boxers with a hand and moved sideways into my room to put on my shorts. I pulled out the waist belt that made me uncomfortable. It was a nuisance having to dress up at home. I washed my face and went to sit down at the breakfast table. Lian had saved a seat for me, as usual. Dad peered down at my legs as I sat on the bench next to her.

Lian elbowed me, as if by accident. "Brother and I are going to swim in the afternoon."

"Not today," I said. "I'm going to see a friend of mine."

"Don't leave your sister out," Mom said. "You've spent plenty of time with your friends during the school year. Now take a break from them—that's what summer is for."

Dad nodded. "Jiang Jieshi was married at fifteen, your age,

60

son. Likewise, you should be taking some family responsibilities."

Lian grinned so wide that her front teeth protruded from her lips. I fixed my eyes on my porridge and tried to think.

"It's not like you'll let me get married," I said.

"What I meant is the level of personal maturity." Dad scanned the table, but it was clear he was talking to me. "You should grow not only physically but also mentally and psychologically."

Sometimes I thought Dad's being a psychology professor made him a little uptight. Not that he really knew what was going on with me. He didn't let me read Freud's book and said the translation was poor. One day I skimmed a few pages of *The Ego and the Id* and found many instances of "penis" and "phallus." I read that it wasn't unnatural for a man to wake up in the morning with an erection. Honestly I had read a few banned books that were way better than Freud's. My favorite was *The Desire of a Virgin,* in which the girl yearns to make clouds and rain with her cousin. I'd also read *The Story of Golden Lotus,* but the adultery bored me, and the murder was gross.

Lian swung her legs back and forth and made our bench totter. I told my parents, "I'd better get back to my geometry book," and left the table. I took my bowl to my room. It was a relief not to see Lian, even for a short while.

Mom stopped her from following me. "Now eat your breakfast like a young lady. Let your brother study on his own."

I shut my door to block out the rest of their conversation.

Alone in my room, I reminisced about my first "date" with Zhou three years ago. I had slipped out of a soccer game during PE class. A girl on the school's swim team, I forgot her name, had enlightened us boys that the girls could be excused from

61

their PE classes during their menstrual periods. I knew my mom had periods, but I was curious to find out *who* was having them in my class and took a rest from PE. Heading back to the classroom building, I planned on grabbing an unlucky girl's pencil box and making her run after me. I was a good runner. I could slow down if she fell behind. If she got too close, I would jump out of the windows and watch if she'd jump, too. I wouldn't give her back the pencil box until she begged me or threatened to tell the teacher.

All the windows were open. At first I saw no one in the classroom. Then I heard low sobbing and found Zhou alone. Just the girl I wouldn't mess with. I almost wanted to run back to the soccer game. Instead I peeked in. Her silky hair was tied in a ponytail with a white ribbon, and she wore a white dress with a red belt. She looked like a lotus fairy, grown out of silt but untainted. Whatever she was crying about, I felt I had to help her.

I entered the classroom, bumped hard into a desk, and groaned loudly, "Oww!"

She lifted her head. Her face was so soft and perfect that it broke my heart to see her red eyes. But I kept my face down and pretended not to notice her tears.

"Are you all right?" she asked. Her voice was melodious, a little hoarse from crying.

I stood in a crouch, my hand still gripping my side. "The desk attacked me." I stole a glance at her.

She smiled, wiped her cheeks, and smiled some more. "You should be careful," she said. "Desks don't attack people."

I limped to her desk. "So how are you?" I asked. "Are you taking a break?"

"Not really." She wiped the tear-wrinkled page of her notebook. "Our math teacher asked me to do geometry exercises, but I don't know how." She looked up at me and I was afraid she'd cry again, but she didn't. "I feel so stupid," she said.

I peered at her exercises. "No, this is hard stuff," I told her. "Do you mind if I give it a try?"

"Oh, please," she said. "Please."

I knew the solutions at first glance, but I went out of my way to make a number of rough drafts, before finally slapping my forehead and saying, "I got it." I wrote it out rapidly, then explained it to her three times before I saw the light of understanding on her face.

"You're so good, and so smart. Now I can go see the teacher, and he won't pull my hair." She put her hands behind her head to tighten her ponytail.

"What's that mark?" I pointed my finger at the side of her cheek, careful not to touch her creamy skin.

"Nothing."

"But there's a pink mark. Can't you look in the window for yourself?"

She unlatched the window frame and pulled it close to her face. "I didn't know he pinched so hard." She kneaded her face with her palm.

"How could he hurt you? You should tell your parents."

"No." She twisted her fingers for some time. "My dad would pull me out of school if I did. He tried so hard to get me in here."

She sounded so afraid that I could only ask, "Does your dad beat you at home?"

"Never. Sometimes he sighs and gives me a look that goes all the way into my heart." She laid her forehead back on her arms and said to the floor, "I'm such a failure."

I almost blurted out: how could you be a failure when you're so beautiful and talented? Her solo singing had been broadcast on campus. "Don't kid me, you're a thousand times better than I've ever been." I tried to sound at ease. "I was the naughtiest boy on the whole block. Both my sisters were teachers' pets, while I, the son, was everyone's worst nightmare. Not until middle school did I begin to catch up." I stopped, lest I should tell her about the spankings that I had gotten. I said enough to become her friend, the only friend she could turn to for help with math problems during these past three years.

A loud thud on my door made me start. "Brother, do you want your drawing compasses back?" I wondered if Lian had bumped my door with her shoulder.

I put my feet on the crossbar of my desk. "Go away" or "Keep it" was on the tip of my tongue. Instead, I stood up and opened the door for her.

She slipped inside like a fish swimming into a net. "Can I borrow your multi-ruler?"

I sat on my bed, waiting for her to find what she needed in my drawer. She took out my plastic ruler and peered at me for my reaction.

I shrugged and told her, "Take it."

"Thank you." She passed me on her way out.

I said to her back, "Remember that I can't take you swimming today. I have to go see a friend of mine."

She stopped. "Who?"

I stood up to lean on the door. "What's that to you?"

She drew a half-circle with the ruler in her hand. "Maybe I know him."

I shut the door in her face. She thought my friend had to be a guy—how childish she was! I wondered if she pestered me so much because I was the only male friend she had. Not that I had showed her any affection that was beyond mere tolerance.

I grabbed my dad's red tie on my way out. But I couldn't quite figure out how to wear it. I wound it this way and that, and tied such a fat knot that it nearly choked me. I pulled it loose and retied it. Finally I was able to walk without feeling like I was wearing a dog leash.

At Zhou's apartment, I pressed the doorbell. As I waited, I straightened my shirt. My tie was too wide for my chest. I liked how it looked on my dad but I had forgotten how much bigger he was. I should've worn a long-sleeved shirt and buttoned up its sleeves, instead of showing my skinny arms.

The door opened and Zhou's mother appeared. "Mrs. Yan?" I stammered. "My name is Wei. I'm Zhou's classmate. I came by to see if she's read the geometry quiz book. It's hard." I hoped she would ignore my excuse and take me to see Zhou.

As she looked me up and down, I clasped my hands behind my back so that she couldn't see them shaking. Finally, crow's feet bloomed around her eyelids as she broke into a smile.

"Come on in," she said.

I didn't know what I expected to see inside, but I was disappointed to find how bland and neat it was. Except for the poster on her door, there was no sign this was the home of a teen star. The sycamore tree leaves cast a shadow on the windows. The only sound I heard was children playing in the streets. I started when Mrs. Yan put down a tall glass of sour plum juice on the table.

"Looks like you could use a drink." She pushed a napkin toward me. "So you're the math whiz Zhou talked about. Your mom must be proud of you."

I wiped my sweaty hands on my pants.

"Maybe you haven't heard. Zhou's tour was extended because she was so well received in the concerts. She'll travel with the art troupe and return to school in the fall."

I choked on my own saliva and coughed. Then I lifted the glass to drink some plum juice. In a hurry I swallowed an ice cube, which got stuck in my lower throat. I took another drink to wash down the ice cube. The juice tasted like sour medicine in my mouth.

"It's better for Zhou that she can sing." Mrs. Yan lowered her voice as if to confide a secret. "Zhou is not good at math like you. School has been hard on her."

"She has a talent." I would never put Zhou down, especially to her own mother. "She's better than me."

Mrs. Yan fixed her eyes on me. "Are you interested in her autographed poster?"

I shook my head. What was the use? I already had one.

"Come have a look." Mrs. Yan patted my hand.

She rose to open Zhou's bedroom door, and I followed. "Let me see if there are any left," she said.

I leaned on the doorframe, taking in the neat double bed and ivory throw on the pillow. When Mrs. Yan spread open a poster in front of her, I took a step back.

"Would you like this one?" she asked.

I stroked Zhou's signature with the back of my hand. "It's nice."

She rolled up the poster. "You should come again and see her sometime. She's very fond of you, and I can see why."

Embarrassed by her praise, I bowed deeply to accept the poster. "Thank you, Mrs. Yan. I love to hear her sing."

We said goodbye. I went home carrying a rolled-up poster, feeling empty-handed and hollow inside.

When I took Lian swimming the next day, I felt so depressed I could barely stay afloat. The sound of people's chattering and laughing made my stomach turn. I dove into the deep water in order to have a moment of silence. But I couldn't stay underwater for long and surfaced each time spewing water like a killer whale. Lian asked me what new game I was playing. I told her it was the deep-water dive.

It seemed to be a harmless game. We raced each other to touch the bottom of the pool, starting from the shallow end then moving toward the deeper side. She had a hard time sinking because as a girl, she had more body fat. I snickered at her attempt to wiggle her way down, flip and flop like a fish stuck to the bait.

Soon I left Lian practicing in the shallows and swam to the deepest end by myself, where I saw the girl in my class who was on the swim team. I didn't say hello because she didn't seem to recognize me when I got near. Her face was blank, her eyes looking far away as if at the cloudless sky. Her upper body was wet, her hands holding tightly onto a young man's shoulders. I could only see his muscular back and handsome profile, his face almost touching her stomach. The straps on her swimsuit cut into her tan shoulders.

I rolled my legs forward and made a dive into the water. As my sinking slowed, I opened my eyes and groped at the cement wall of the pool to touch the floor, three-and-a-half meters deep. On the way back up, I saw a forest of legs kicking around me, before I glimpsed two meters from me, an exposed vagina. The bathing suit was pulled aside and pinned to her thigh by a man's bony hand. Her legs opened up like a pair of drawing compasses, while two thick fingers were sliding in and out of her in a frightful rhythm. I saw her sparse pubic hair and pinkish flesh with the brutal fingers inside. I swam away as far as I could, and just before my lungs exploded, I surfaced like a dead fish.

"Where have you been?" Lian's whiny voice broke me from my trance. I found myself back at the shallow end but couldn't remember how I had made it so far in a single breath.

I glared at my chubby sister. Her breasts lifted her swimsuit with plum-sized bumps. I'd seen her bathing countless times before, but only now, with the straps of her swimsuit clamped tightly onto her meaty shoulders, could I picture her vagina, hairy and pink, and how she might open her own legs like a pair of drawing compasses for fingers to slide in and out.

She pinched her nose and yelled, "Look at me!" and made a back flip into the water. Her white feet were the last I saw of her before she disappeared into the water.

After a few seconds, she popped out of the water. "Darn!" she said.

"What's wrong?"

"I'm deaf." She tossed her head to make water bounce off her hair. For no reason, I reached out and stroked her head so lightly that she barely noticed.

On our way home, I walked behind her as she hopped like a baby sparrow in order to shake the water from her ears.

"I'm tired, brother." She resumed walking. "My period does that to me. I'll take a week off." I shrugged, and she raised her voice. "Aren't you going to jump for joy?"

At night, alone in my room, I took out Zhou's autographed poster to spread it on my bamboo mat. I stroked the signature across her belly. How chaste she looked in her white gown, although the smile on her lips seemed to be mocking my naïveté. After all that reading on making clouds and rain, I had to witness the act in a public pool in order to understand how a man makes love to his girlfriend. How awkward it was, and yet how exciting it must be! Perhaps one day Zhou would want me to make love to her, like a real man. I must not disappoint her. I couldn't afford to take a chance, not with her. Maybe with other girls, I could. But I wasn't going to risk falling in love with any other girl, just because I needed to learn about the female body—what it wants, and what makes it happy.

Now I felt grateful that Zhou had been delayed on the road and given me time to learn about lovemaking before we would meet again. I should practice my strokes on a girl because, without the physical act, love was just pretty words and the same pathetic crush that went nowhere.

I bent down to kiss the signature across her belly and licked the shadow between her legs where her gown draped. It tasted of dry paper and rancid ink, where my saliva smudged her writing. I reached out a hand to the pendant light and nudged the lampshade to make the yellow beam sweep up and down her body, my heart swinging behind my ribcage and rising and falling like waves.

On Sunday night we gathered in front of the television as usual to watch *Wu Zetian,* the story of the woman emperor. I hid the remote control under my stool. When the commercials began, Lian wanted to take a peek at the local talent show, and Dad insisted on catching a glimpse of the news.

I put the remote control in Lian's hand. "Go ahead."

She choked on her words with her mouth open. "Oh." She touched the remote as if it were fake.

Dad said, "Channel 5, the news is almost over."

Lian switched to the channel where the talent show was on.

"What's up with you?" Dad asked me.

"You taught me Jiang Jieshi was married at my age."

Mom burst into a broad smile. "You should be happy, old man. Our son is learning to take care of his sister."

Dad patted the back of my head. "You could've picked some other time." He slapped a palm fan against his shins to drive away mosquitoes. "You know Jiang Jieshi was later divorced and married a younger woman."

"Even so," Mom said. Her fingers moved two bamboo needles back and forth to knit a bundle of yellow yarn into a sweater for me.

I was relieved to see Lian back at the pool after a week of having her period. We raced to the deep end and had three diving contests in a row. I was dumb enough to let her win them all. She grew a little bored and pouted.

"Why can't you dive today, brother?"

"I don't know. You seem to be getting better."

"How is that possible?" She brushed the wet hair off of her face to the back of her ears. "I haven't practiced at all for seven days." I noticed the thin hair in her armpits when she lifted both her arms.

"Maybe that's what makes you better," I lied. My heart began to pump so hard inside my ribcage that I was afraid she might see it protrude.

"You mean, my period?" She paddled so close that she was almost breathing on me. "I don't suppose so. I can't take PE classes when I'm having my period, you know."

"Right." I nodded, feeling stupid. "Maybe the fact that you have that, I mean, that you're a girl, makes diving easier for you."

"Really?" Her eyelids crinkled with a smile, and I watched her as if watching myself smile. "Do you admit I'm a better diver?" she asked.

I breathed in hard. "What I mean is, that you're a girl, you have what I don't have, which is an advantage." I patted her behind casually.

"All right." She lifted her chin to me like a play-acting queen. "I accept your bow to my supremacy."

I paddled to her other side. She was getting obnoxious. "Do you know what really makes you a girl?" I stared into her eyes. "Maybe you haven't heard; one day, a man can use your thing to make you happy. It's called 'to please you.' Don't you want to know what it feels like?"

She threw her head back, breaking into a loud laugh as if one of us had lost his mind. But I was too hotheaded to be afraid of her, a young girl. "What do I have to do?" she asked.

Obviously she didn't believe me and was eager to prove me wrong.

"Just open your legs a little, and hold onto my shoulders, if you like." She did it, and I groped her round bottom. Her bathing suit tightened when I pulled its crotch aside.

"Ouch, it's choking me."

"Sorry." I touched her pussy on the front and she giggled.

"You're tickling me," she said. "Can you not tickle me?"

I thumbed the layers of her pussy, hesitating.

"What're you trying to do?" she asked.

I held her up a little closer, then began to push a finger in.

"Ouch, your fingernail." She shoved me aside and pulled her bathing suit in place. "I don't want to play anymore. You can't 'please' me."

She swam back to the shallow end so I didn't get to touch her again. I rolled my legs backward to dive into the water, and bumped my head hard on the cement wall. All voices were reduced to a wordless drone. I pressed my head with both hands, kicking frantically to surface. For once, I was afraid of drowning.

Lian stayed in my room when Mom put a bandage on my head. The leg of the drawing compasses rolled crisply on the glass top of my desk as Lian drew circles overlapping circles on a sheet of paper.

Mom pressed a stripe of adhesive tape under my hairline. "Be careful, son, don't get it wet for a couple of days." She took her first-aid box and left.

Lian walked to me and poked my bandage with the end of her drawing compasses. I moaned.

"You're a casualty," she said.

I cupped my bandage to shield myself from her attack. She returned to my desk.

"I'll tell Mom and Dad about what you did to me, unless—"

"What?" I interrupted her.

"Unless you're nice to me."

She found a penny in my drawer and covered it with a piece of paper, then smudged her pencil across the white paper until the shape of the coin's inscription emerged.

"You owe me, brother," she muttered.

How on earth had I come up with the stupid scheme without even thinking about the trouble Lian could bring me? But I had no use for regrets. I jumped up to press the eject key on my cassette player.

"Didn't you want this?" I put Zhou's tape in her hand. "You can have it."

"If you were my legend," she read and turned the tape over. "Let it be as enduring as the universe."

"Don't tell anyone, and we'll stay friends." I took Zhou's autographed poster from under my bed to spread it on the bamboo mat. "If you don't tell for the whole summer, she's yours, too. It's her authentic ink."

She lifted her hand to touch the signature across Zhou's belly, then pulled back her hand suddenly as if scorched by a heated iron.

I rolled up the poster and put it in her hands. "Mom and Dad won't mind it if you hang it inside your mosquito net, because Zhou is a girl, like you."

For a while she didn't speak. Then she clasped her hands over her mouth and giggled so hard that her shoulders shook.

For the rest of that summer, whenever I was mean to her, Lian threatened to tell our parents about me touching her privates. She never told on me, partly because she liked me, but mostly because she wanted me to like her back. She enrolled in a physiology class when school started, and never mentioned it again. So it has remained our secret ever since.

妹—What the Younger Daughter Once Aspired To . . .

THE MATCH

Our first flop drill for the high jump went easily. At Fei's whistle for the break, all the girls on the junior team tumbled onto the great mattress, piling on one another and wiping our sweat onto each other's skin. Fei carried the foam cooler from the shade into the midday sun and passed each of us a red bean popsicle. As I wolfed mine down, a blob of sherbet fell on my shorts and stained the white print of "Nanjing Juvenile Jumpers Summer Camp." Then I saw Stumpy's shaven head near the long jump pit and leapt off the mattress.

"Stumpy!" I shouted.

It was our turn to practice the long jump, but the sand in the pit was stamped solid with the footprints of the boys. Stumpy and I were in charge of the sand pits this week. If he was going to use the pit, why couldn't he shovel the sand for once? Luckily he jogged back to fetch his spiked shoes by the pit.

"Don't yell. I'm right here." He stooped to grab his shoes, while I peered down at his greenish skull.

"Have you laid a finger on the shovel this whole week? I'm getting calluses from picking up after you." I thrust the shovel into the sand.

"Don't blame me. I saw you do pushups on the parallel bars." He moved his hand up and down the wooden handle to make a light noise. "Hear it? My calluses are harder than yours."

"You've probably always had them," I said.

Stumpy had grown up on a farm. He might've been toiling in the rice field with his parents had he not joined the summer camp. Now he hated chores as much as any boy in his obnoxious bunch.

"You might've been born with them." I regretted this as soon as I heard myself say it.

"I was born as good as you, Pigtail." Stumpy rubbed his bald head as if it were some kind of trophy. "I can high-jump 1.6 meters, ten centimeters more than my height."

"That's because you're short!" I burst into nervous laughter.

"Wrong again. I mastered a secret weapon." When he did a backbend, his shirt slid down his chest to expose his flat nipples. "What's your record, Pigtail?"

"I can jump over 1.52 meters on a good day," I lied. My record was 1.45.

"What do you say we have a match after the practice? You shoot for 1.52 and I do 1.6. The winner can keep their hands off the shovel forever."

Fei was leading our team to the pit, so I had to decide. There would be no real loss for me since I never could coax Stumpy into picking up the shovel.

"Deal. After the practice, just you and me." I wanted to beat Stumpy, but if I didn't, I would hate to let Fei see me lose. "No coaches," I added.

"See you, Pigtail." He jogged away barefooted, carrying his shoes.

"Five thirty, Gourd Head." I pulled out the shovel to dig the sand.

"The key in the triple jump," Fei said, "is to maintain high speed during all three takeoffs—the hop, the step, and the jump—while applying a large driving force with the arms. During the step, keep a tall, upright posture and ride out the flight phase." She made a sharp dash, scratching the dirt with the spikes of her shoes. "Don't hurry the foot back to the ground, but wait for the ground to come to meet your foot. Like this."

She strode, with each step longer and faster than the last, before she took off from the board with a powerful kick and a single-arm thrust into the hop, the step, then a double-arm lift that propelled her into a long flight over the pit, landing her in the sand with her ponytail splashed on her back. I never had a doubt that Fei, with her grace alone, had led me to brave the jumping events.

The first time I had seen Fei, five months ago, I was dazzled by the white stripes on her sky-blue uniform and the matching headband that set off the coral of her cheeks. I had started running toward her, even before she picked up the shiny whistle that hung down from her collar.

"Are you a high jumper?" she had asked me.

"No," I stammered. "Not yet."

"Do you want to give it a try?" Her face bloomed into a perfect smile. "You may be good material."

By the age of fourteen I had had PE teachers tempting me to try long-distance running, swimming, gymnastics, basketball, and volleyball. But that was the first time anyone saw me as a jumper. A coward I wasn't, but I hated to risk tangling up my legs in a bamboo bar and crashing down on my back in the wood shavings.

Fei led us to the high jump pit where two giant mattresses lay, like the ones that we had seen used in the national events on TV. She did a backbend to grab her own ankles, then lunged forward to press her face to her shins. She jogged to the pit and lifted her body like it had just enough weight to be perfect, and flew over the crossbar. Scattered clapping rose. Her whistle caught the light, when she bounced up from the mattress. She was striking, like no other coach at this school. Five months later I followed Fei to the summer camp, hoping that her glory would rub off on me.

Stumpy hopped over the crossbar like a puppy being tossed out of a window.

"What's that?" I rubbed my eyes. "It's the ugliest thing I ever saw!"

"It's the great straddle." He squatted in the pit to lower the bar for me. "How low do your scissors drop, Pigtail?"

I was still panting from my last jump, which I had barely made at 1.42 meters. I kicked my wobbly legs and felt like calling it a day. But I didn't want Stumpy to feel smug.

"I might top 1.52 with the flop," I insisted, "if I had the mattresses."

"Isn't this good enough for you?" He hopped on the wood shavings with hands locked behind his back. "This is practically a cushion!"

I paced around the pole. "Have you heard of the princess and the pea, bumpkin?"

He fell on his butt with his legs spread apart. "What is that?"

"Once upon a time, there was a very beautiful and delicate princess, who slept on top of seven thick quilts with a pea at the bottom. The next day she was bruised all black and blue by that tiny pea, which proved she was a real princess."

He glared at me as if a toad had fallen out of my mouth. "But you're not a princess!" he scolded. "You're a high jumper. A princess doesn't wear pigtails!"

Convinced that the offense was his, not mine, I turned to walk toward my dorm.

"I can teach you the straddle," he called after me. "Then you can be my partner at the mixed jumping event."

But it was two weeks away. Pin, my roommate, had talked about teaming with Stumpy—"the Champ," as she called him. I wondered why she wanted to win so badly.

"If you let me teach you the straddle, you'll win," he shouted louder.

I stopped. Was he being generous? I turned around with my hands on my hips.

"It's easy. Run very fast, and just before takeoff, get as slow as possible. Give your lead leg a full swing to clear the crossbar. Think of it as a big quick hop. Let me show you." He ran up and rolled over the bar like a cat, dropping onto the wood shavings. "Your turn." He knelt in the pit on both knees.

I eyed the crossbar, at a height I had not braved before, and took a deep breath. As I jogged toward the pit, I began to worry about what to do with my legs. I tried to lift my left leg as I did in the scissors but slipped on the ground, stumbling into the pit with a frightened scream.

I heard him say, "Focus on your legs, not the crossbar! You almost made it!"

"The straddle isn't for everyone," Fei said and lifted the towel from my bandaged knee. "You need a great deal of leg strength. I can see why it's Stumpy's cup of tea, but you? You have the light build for the flop." She rubbed her warm hands down my thigh.

I got goosebumps watching her long fingers run down my shin, ankle, and foot, and would've fallen into her arms if she hadn't tickled my sole.

"How does that feel?" she asked.

"Even better than the popsicle," I said. My injury might be a blessing in disguise after all.

She brushed back a strand of hair that fell over my eyes. I wanted to both wince and bend forward to prolong her touch.

"Will you feel lonely on the bench by yourself?" she asked.

I heard crickets chirping and frogs croaking outside—the sound of contentment in the evening air. Pin had washed my bowls and spoon before she left for a movie. My throat felt tight as I reflected on my wretched condition.

"Let me see what I can do." Fei wrapped a towel gently around my knee. "Would you like to meet my daughter tomorrow?"

My leg jerked as if stung by a bee. "Your. . . ." I cleared my throat.

"She's almost two years old and doesn't like being in the daycare. I was afraid I couldn't watch her as I coached. But with the extra help of your good eyes, you'll set my mind at ease." She crossed her arms.

"Sure."

I wasn't able to pull my eyes away from her tan arms folded on her lemon-dotted sleeveless dress. She looked tidy and crisp, not much older than I was. How could I have guessed that Fei had been made pregnant by a man?

The next day I limped to the playground and found a little girl in white overalls sitting on the parallel bars.

Pin nudged me and asked, "Isn't her daughter pretty?"

She was the tiniest thing I had seen in a while, with a spotless face, big eyes, and a small mouth. Her long eyelashes seemed fit only to be on a Barbie doll, but she was all real, fleshy, and shy.

"Mommy." She wrinkled her nose as if she'd cry.

"It's okay, baby." Fei rocked her back and forth while pointing at us. "See the big sisters? You're going to play and have fun."

Pin whispered to me, "Fei must've cut off her daughter's eyelashes to make them grow longer."

"What if they didn't grow back?" I was horrified.

"A baby's eyelashes always grow back longer," Pin said. "You have to do it when the baby is asleep, though."

Fei blew her whistle and nudged her daughter toward me. I took hold of her little shoulder. Thumb in her mouth, she watched Fei lead the team to the jumping pit in the grass field.

"Mommy." She pointed.

"Isn't she pretty? And she made you such a cutie." I touched her eyelashes with the side of my finger. "Do you know she cut off your lashes when you were asleep? My mom never did that when I was little. There's no catching up for that, you know?"

She blinked and grabbed my finger. This soft bundle of Fei's flesh—what an enviable miracle she was!

"Do you know she *made* you?" I whispered into her ear.

Fei blew a whistle for the team to do the single-leg bounds. Her wavy ponytail dipped to the blue elastic band of her shorts every time she nodded. I thought she was too lovely to be a mother. I could've glanced at my mom or our neighbor Mrs. Wang and guessed they were mothers. Their bobbed hair was permed into fat curls, their faces glowed with vanishing cream, and they wore tunics covering their ample hips. Even so, the bulges of their stomachs startled me the few times I bumped into them. Fei was trim and flat-chested, but a mother after all; she had gotten naked with her husband to become pregnant with this girl. I wondered if she had felt awkward about undressing in front of him for the first time, or if she simply couldn't wait to do it.

The girl pointed again. "Mommy's playing."

I stroked her soft arm. "Where is your daddy, cutie?"

"Daddy takes train."

"What do you mean?"

"Daddy takes train." She blew bubbles with her drool.

I hugged her and kissed the side of her neck. She smelt of milk. Was it Fei's, too? Fei peered at us with a smile. Suddenly I blushed to the roots of my hair.

I had to take my big brother Wei to lunch the next day, after he brought me a bag of lychees from home. He was reluctant to sit on the girls' side of the canteen. I told him it was the plump fruits in the string bag that attracted the other boys' gazes. When Pin put down her chopsticks, I pressed four lychees into her palm.

"Guess who I saw yesterday on the street," Pin said. "A fellow riding a bicycle and carrying Fei on the backseat and her girl on the front. He's a knockout, too, a nice match for her."

"Does the baby look like him?" I asked.

"She has his mouth and eyes, I guess." She spat the lychee pit into her enamel bowl, which bounced with a dull echo. "Her eyelashes may be extra long, you know?"

I nodded with a smile.

My brother stabbed a piece of pork with his chopsticks. "Your canteen isn't bad," he said.

I lowered my face when I glimpsed Stumpy walking toward us. "I know."

"Hello, are you Lian's brother?" Stumpy reached out his hand to shake Wei's. "Your sister is a good jumper."

"Yeah?" Wei's face lit up. "Are you the little guy who did the straddle?"

"They call me Stumpy." He lifted his leg. "Look at my muscles. I used to jump over the hay. Landing in wood shavings is like a cushion to me." Stumpy didn't look at me. "Are you a jumper, too?" he asked Wei.

"No, but I like to swim." Wei grabbed a handful of lychees to give to Stumpy. "Maybe I'll become a diver."

I sneered. Who knew what he would do in a pool? Wei and

I had gone swimming together years ago. One day he had talked me into letting him touch my privates. When I felt his hard fingernail pushing in, I got mad and swam away. I hadn't told my parents about it—what was the point in getting him beaten for a thing past? But it never passed with me. I still remembered the feel of his nail bruising my thing, and was shocked at what a dirty trick a boy could play on a girl.

Pin scooped the broken shells into her bowl and dusted her hands. "Do you know Fei and her husband are a long-distance couple?"

"What does that mean?" I asked.

"They live apart until school breaks. Her husband teaches at a high school in Shanghai that has a pilot program for teenage male high jumpers. . . ."

I couldn't help overhearing Stumpy boast about his straddle skill to Wei. "It's the only thing I've learned here, man. Coach said I was built for the straddle, see what I mean?" He showed off his shin again. "So I was excited to show your sister." He blushed briefly. "What I didn't know then was how to teach a novice. . . ."

How dare he call me a novice to my brother and behind my back! We hadn't talked since my fall, and he couldn't make amends with me like this. I threw the spoon in my enamel bowl to make a loud noise.

Stumpy went on as if he hadn't heard me. "She worries about the crossbar more than her lead leg. That's not right. The number one rule in high jump is always focusing on your run-up and takeoff, never the crossbar, or you're sure to lose count of your own steps, you know what I mean?"

"I see why you joined the summer camp." Wei winked at me. "For peer advice like this, right?"

I surprised myself by saying, "Advice my ass," pushed away from the table, and stormed off. Pin didn't follow me. Halfway across the room, I dashed back to fetch my lychees.

I heard Wei tell Stumpy, "Don't mind my bossy sister."

Fei lifted her arms and right leg. "As you move from run to takeoff, you must convert horizontal speed into a large vertical impulse. Loading the takeoff is the key, because once you leave the ground, very little can be done in the air."

Fei's daughter raised her head to fall back into my arms. She was already imitating Fei's moves with striking accuracy, and she was fearless, even with me. I had been feeling down ever since Stumpy offered his advice—to Wei, of all people! Luckily Pin was on the bench with me, because it was the heaviest day of her period.

"Your brother is cute," Pin said.

I was shocked. "He is *not*! He's the slacker in my family."

"Slacker who?" Pin elbowed me. "He took a two-hour bus trip to bring you the lychees, and you walked out on him at lunch."

"It's not all my fault. Right, baby?" I flung her chubby arms about, and she giggled. "Would you like me to braid your hair?" I held her face in my palms. "You'll be so pretty."

She gripped my knees and mumbled, "Pretty, yes!"

I parted her fine hair at the top of the crown into three equal parts. I was so absorbed in my job that I didn't notice Fei walking near.

"Were you two listening to my flop drill?" Fei rubbed her daughter's head to make the strands of hair slip through my fingers. "I'm expecting you to return and perform in the final events."

Pin nodded. I just stared at Fei. She didn't have to fuss over the drill with me. After all, I was only a student who babysat her daughter.

"How's your knee?"

I kicked up my foot. "Kind of stiff."

She tapped my knee with a finger. "It's because you haven't been training."

I wished she hadn't touched me so callously. I watched her face for the clues that her husband was in town, that she was sleeping with him every night—a thing like that must show itself on a spotless face, but there was nothing obvious. I never knew love could be so invisible and ordinary.

"We have two kinds of popsicles," Fei said. "What would you girls like?"

"A red bean," Pin said.

"I want milk." I blushed.

While Fei carried the foam cooler to the mattresses to feed the other girls, I told Pin, "I'm going to retire after this. Stumpy was right—I'm not jumper material."

She licked her popsicle. "He didn't mean it like that."

"I can't out-jump Stumpy. So what? It's only a crossbar." I bounced Fei's daughter straddling my lap. "I bet your mom does the flop style way prettier than your dad." I straightened my legs to lay the girl's head upside down upon my shins, as she giggled nervously.

Pin stood up to take hold of the girl's waist.

"Slowly." I slid her down my good leg. "Do you still want to team up with Stumpy?" I asked Pin.

She winked at me. "If he'll have me."

"I can help you with that." I chewed my popsicle. "But I want him to be my partner at the bonfire party afterwards."

She tilted her head. "Does the party carry points?"

"No," I said. "Points aren't everything." She stared at me, and I elbowed her. "Watch your popsicle—it's melting!"

At the bonfire party, I am one of the few girls who wear dresses. My rayon dress with yellow sunflowers on black cloth feels like it's pouring down my skin. Pin wears the souvenir shirt for a mixed-jump finalist and sits on the bench with her back to us. I've said nothing to Stumpy about their losing the final, which, to me, was no loss at all. I tap the stone I sit on with the heels of my plastic sandals and dance to my own cheery beat. Then Fei asks us to tell our partners what led us to join the summer camp.

"For the fun of the game." Stumpy squints at me, while I feel the warmth of fire on my thigh. "My brain never works better than when I stand in front of the crossbar and know exactly how I'm going to clear it." He pushes down my knee to stop my leg from kicking. "Your turn."

I think of Fei, her flight over the bar, her long-lashed daughter who isn't afraid of letting me catch her fall, her handsome husband whom she loves more than us, possibly—the three of them balancing on the same bicycle. It seems silly to confess how Fei once held me spellbound.

I chuckle and tease Stumpy, "For the match with you."

He glares at me. "What're you talking about?"

"The old saying is right—out of blows, friendship grows." I toss my head and burst into a loud laugh. "That's us, right?"

It begins to rain so we retreat to our dorms. A paper plane flies out of the opposite boys' building, wheeling in the air for a few minutes before it crashes to the ground. Several new planes drift out into the moist evening air. One veers into the neighboring window. Another is sticking to the wall and unwilling to leave. A few plunge into the gathering puddles while their makers yell, "Come back here!"

Only one plane crosses the road, making its way toward our windows. The boys' cheering and shouting might have moved the plane, had it not been made of paper. When it hits our wall and drops off, a deep sigh rises in unison from both dorms.

I run downstairs to reclaim the plane and hold it up like a trophy.

姊—How the Older Daughter Looks . . .

THE HOMELY GIRL

I haven't thought about my looks until this train trip home. Ting tells me the salon street in Nanjing has expanded into a fashion district with clothing stores and beauty parlors that follow the trends in Shanghai.

She waves her *Fashion Monthly* at me. "I don't think she's that pretty."

I look at the model she's pointing to, a skinny girl with large black eyes. "Well, she has pretty eyes."

She puts the picture at arm's length, then moves it close to her own eyes. "I think not."

A young man across the aisle looks at Ting. She is a beautiful girl. She has what my mom calls proportional features, something I haven't inherited. The man's eyes linger on her chest then move away. From a distance, he may not be able to make out the school badge pinned to her ivory blouse with the burgundy fine print that reads Shanghai University. I wear one, too, on my cotton dress. If I had a silk blouse like Ting's, I would hate to ruin it with the badge. Ting told me that after she first wore it, she had to always fasten the school badge in the two pinholes on her blouse.

Her hair waves in the wind against the fast-moving green fields outside the train window. Ting already has a good-looking boyfriend but doesn't want to take him home just yet. She still drags me along to clothing shops. With her I've bought a new coat, not yet any skirts. It's my first college summer.

"Guess what, Rou?" she says.

I push up my glasses on my nose.

"Research shows wearing earrings may benefit your eyesight," she reads from the magazine. "There is a higher percentage of people who do not need corrective lenses among earring wearers."

"Learn something every day," I reply.

Our train speeds by billboards of headshots that feature chubby-cheeked provincial beauties with bright-eyed dimpled smiles. We're entering Nanjing now. I've been away for a year, and the station hasn't changed the ads. It's the same unfashionable hometown as when I left. I'm almost home, but I'm not ready.

"Will you do me a favor, Ting?" I ask.

"Anything for you, lady, my honor entirely." She puts her slim hand on her chest.

"Well, it's no big deal. Just, you see, shall we stop by the salon street?"

Her eyes open wide. Is she acting dumb? I try to smile.

"You mean, now?" she asks.

"Yeah." I nod hastily. "Yeah."

She rises with a smile. No wonder I love her. My best friend asks no questions.

Out of the train station into the hot sun, we each drag two travel bags on our beauty quest. "I'll check out bathing suits, maybe a two-piece," Ting says. We get on the bus, and she begins to take off her school badge. A few people are watching her.

"What're you doing?" I ask.

"So we don't get ripped off," she explains. "Haven't you shopped there before?"

I haven't. "Students may have discounts," I guess.

"Sure. They'll double the prices, then give you 15 percent off. You don't want to show them your parents are paying."

Where has she learned the ins and outs? A year ago, no, two months ago, before she started dating, she was simple like me. Now she talks like a cosmopolitan woman. I take off my badge and find a young man studying the two pinholes on Ting's blouse.

"What do you want?" Ting asks.

"Oh, anything." I stoop to look at my reflection in the windows. "To show that I've been at the university for a whole year, you know?"

She nods. "Get yourself a pair of contacts."

"You think so?"

"Why not?"

Why not. I blink, watching my eyes inside the yellow plastic frames that have faded to clear. Six years ago I took my mother's advice to heart, thereby relinquishing my own personal style.

"Looks don't matter," Mom said.

I was thirteen, trying on my new glasses at home. I saw my face in the mirror, drooping under the weight of the frame.

"The glasses hide your bulging eyes," she said.

I turned my face to her. She seemed farther than usual, smaller, her eyes so keen they startled me. I felt the floor floating up when I moved my eyes away from her.

"The glasses make your nose look daintier." She sighed. "You have your father's nose."

I stood up from my chair, put my foot down lightly for every step, and gripped the edge of the table as I moved toward her side. She looked at the photos spread on the table. I sat down in a chair by her, looking at her profile, the eyes and nose that I hadn't inherited.

"Can you help?" She wanted to send four of our baby photos to be enlarged and colored. She had chosen three, one of mine, one of my brother's, one of my sister's, and was looking for the fourth.

I pushed the glasses back up my nose. "I feel dizzy."

"Okay, Rou." She pardoned me from the chore. She picked up my brother's photo, taken when he was five years old, holding a toy machine gun. "Wei has my nose and eyes. Look at those dimples, bigger than coins!" She traced the lovely dents with her pinky. "They all say that's a sign of good fortune. He had the prettiest baby teeth too, like little grains of rice. When he smiled, his eyes curved like two half-moons. And his complexion was so. . . ." She finally ran out of words, holding the black-and-white photo in her palm. It had to be her last pick and, no doubt, her favorite.

I sat up to look at my face in the armoire mirror. It was a

little warped, showing a narrow face I found I liked. I was on the chubby side for a girl, Mom once told me, but luckily I had an okay complexion.

"Peachy?" I said.

"Yes, peachy." She wasn't satisfied. "It was almost . . . powdery. You know what I mean?"

Wei took all the pretty features from both of my parents, but I wanted what belonged to me, my peachy complexion. The yellow plastic frame made me look pale. I took off my glasses and let the photos in front of me fade into a blur.

Mom glanced at me. "You look better with the glasses, Rou."

So I became stuck with an extra pair of eyes.

I jump off the bus after Ting. My bag hits the back of her legs, and she stumbles. I grab her elbow and ask, "Are you buying a two-piece for *him?*"

She shrugs. "You should think about contacts."

Should I? I just want Mom to think I'm pretty. "Glasses suit me."

She doesn't seem to hear.

"You don't know what a drag it is to adjust to new glasses," I add.

"I said con-tacts."

"Same thing."

She nudges me onto the sidewalk. "If you wish to look homely, four eyes."

I laugh. "Can you blame me? My brother is the pretty one." My face grows warm.

"Prettier than *you?*" she asks in such an oily voice that I stare at her.

"Of course," I say. "He's a boy. A boy can be much prettier than a girl."

"Nonsense." She pulls out her arm from mine and walks ahead.

I take long strides to catch up. "I didn't make it up, Ting."

Homely is a sharp word. What does she know about being plain? Besides, she's an only daughter of doting parents.

You see, Ting, my mom doted on my brother because he was pretty. Dad said Wei was both pretty and thoughtless. They said little about me, except that I was a sensible girl, the last thing I wanted to hear. I didn't want to be a goodie-goodie, while my brother was as wild as he could be. I wanted to be like him—I didn't want to be left out. It didn't matter that he got attention with pettiness and bad manners. Like the day I went to the kitchen and saw his face buried in a wedge of watermelon. I sat on the bench and watched him eat. I never had an appetite like his. He was thin and small in his class, even after he had stayed behind to repeat a year's work. I was two years older, three grades higher, a quarter of a meter taller, and fifteen kilos heavier. I was also stronger and smarter, but none of that mattered as I sat there watching him gulp down watermelon as if he'd just endured a famine.

He lifted his head, showing me a melon seed on his wet cheek, and asked if the cripple, our neighbor who has one leg shorter than the other, was in my class.

I said, "Yeah, what about him?"

"He called me names. You want to help me beat him up?"

"Sure," I said. "Wait, he's tall. He's like, two years older than us." I meant me.

"Why? Did he stay behind, too?"

I held up two fingers. "Twice. And he's calling *you* names!"

"He's stupid." Wei spat out melon seeds as if vomiting on the plate. I envied that, too. "Is that him?" He pointed outside.

I couldn't see whom he was pointing at.

"Let's go." He went out.

I put on my glasses and ran after him. Up the ramp, I found Wei and Li in the sycamore grove. Li had his shorter leg arched in the front, ready to fight. Seeing me arrive, he grabbed onto a tree in order to stand still.

"Cripple!" Wei said.

Li smiled, showing us his strong white teeth. "Blockhead. What're you going to do, wrestle me?" He squinted his girlish eyes.

"Yeah!" Wei said and pushed him.

Li's front leg lifted, and then he leaned forward and pushed Wei, who staggered back several steps. "Go home, baby," Li said. "You too, four-eyes."

That did it. I dashed forward, pried Li's fingers from the tree, and dragged his arm down with my weight. Wei pulled Li's back leg until he lost his balance and fell onto the grassy field, with both of us piling on top of him.

"Let me go!" Li struggled and pulled my hair.

"Will you call me blockhead again, cripple?"

"No, let me go!"

We held him down on the ground for two more minutes, then released him. Li sat up, his pale face flushed, and his clothes wrinkled with dirt stains and pieces of grass in the creases. He looked at Wei, then at me, and broke into a guffaw.

"What?"

He was laughing while we stared at him anxiously for an answer. "Good fight, missy." He threw away a piece of my long hair and scrabbled up, looking at me from head to toe. He made as if to address me, but broke down into another laugh, then turned and limped away on his uneven legs.

"So we won," I tell Ting.

She blinks, trying to grasp my story. "You two beat up a cripple?" she asks.

"We just threw him on the ground. He wasn't hurt or anything."

She says quietly, "Rou, you silly," and bursts into laughter.

"I was thirteen years old. Should I let a cripple bully my brother?"

She laughs until she's gasping and wiping her eyes. Passersby watch her curiously.

"Keep it down, now." I pull her arm to steady her.

"Have you had a boyfriend?" she asks suddenly.

I'm dazed for an instant, wondering what she means. "What do you think?" I sneer at her question. She's only been dating for two months—now all she can think of is a boyfriend.

"I thought so." She touches my arm. "It's good to wait until you're ready, you know, to get physical."

I slap her hand, and she titters. Growing up with my brother made me a tomboy, a part difficult for me to outgrow.

During the long summer I began to dread the hottest nights. My brother never noticed when I grew shy. At sixteen I concealed my anxiety and went along with our family routines.

On one such humid day after dinner, Mom called on me first to take a bath, claiming, "The cleanest tub is saved for the young lady." I shut the windows and pulled down the curtain. Safe from the eyes outside, I shut the bathroom door, alone and naked in my basin.

Mom knocked.

"I'm in here," I said.

Mom opened the door and asked, "Are you sure? In this heat." She had moved our only electric fan into the hallway.

"Okay." I watched the door swing open and bump against the wall. Feeling the breeze on my wet back, I was a little sad but relieved. Hopefully, I consoled myself, the weather would promptly cool down, then I'd be able to close the door reasonably.

Wei was bored by having no one to talk to, so he took a stool to sit down by my basin. I poured water on my arms and splashed him a little. I saw him blink, but he didn't budge.

"Sis, we read this odd poem in class, that Hua Mulan went to the army for her old father."

"For ten years!" I nodded.

"She must be quite a warrior. I wonder what weapon she was best at."

"She could be an archer." I adored sharp eyes.

"Is that in the poem?" he asked.

"No. Yeah. Maybe. . . ."

Mom passed by and said, "Hurry up."

We ignored her, talking about school, books, teachers, discussing one thing after another like two best friends. Whenever I looked at him, his eyes were locked into mine. The electric fan puffed up his hair on the back of his head like a helmet. He was glued to his stool, tracking and debating my words.

I believe my brother heard me perfectly, though he didn't see me at all. No one in my family did, until I left for college.

I stop in front of an earring counter.

The pretty salesgirl waves at me. "Little sister, you'd like to give piercing a try? It doesn't hurt, and it's free if you buy a pair of earrings."

The counter is full of twinkling stars, hearts, and diamond-shaped earrings. "What do you think?" I ask Ting.

"No," she says.

"I want to try it."

She pulls me aside. "Try? They drill holes in your ears. Are you crazy?"

I glance at the two pinholes on her blouse and wonder about the stitches on her lace bra. Then I turn to gaze at the girl's pearl earrings, so lustrous and dazzling. I've never worn jewelry before. Will a pair of earrings look good on me? At least they'll make me the lady to whom Wei is not at all comparable.

"I'd like to have a pair of hearts," I tell the salesgirl and take out my wallet.

She grins and shows me her perfect teeth. "Good choice." She carefully picks out a pair of tiny hearts, holds them to my ear, and hands me a mirror. I look at my face and nod. She marks a dot on each ear. I give the mirror back to the girl.

I sit on the stool and see Ting's serious eyes. I want to smile at her. The girl puts a tiny stapler on my left ear and snaps it through. I feel a sharp sting, then another. I stand up numbly.

"Does it hurt?" Ting asks.

"Not really," I reply.

She looks at me from side to side, nodding lightly. "Hmm."

My head feels light. I hear voices float in the air. I feel pierced, hollow. Ting is walking ahead and I follow her, not knowing where we're going. She glances at the things around her but does not notice how lost I am. I don't want to call out to her.

The bus is coming. She begins to run and I chase after her. We get on the bus, panting. I tilt my head toward the windows and look for the reflection of my golden hearts. I wonder if people see me and think of me as cheeky. A moment ago I was a simple girl who wanted to look pretty to her mother. I remember the woman who sold noodles on the street where we lived. Mom once whispered to me while we were waiting in line, "She's a reformed hooker and, see, she wears earrings." Now I'm the only woman in my family who wears earrings.

The bus jolts, and a man bumps against me. He presses on me for a moment before standing up straight again. I turn to stare at him, but he looks back at me blankly. I recall the young man whom I met at a dance weeks ago. He was tall and muscular, his face handsome and calm. He didn't look at me while we were dancing. He led me quickly and, as we turned, his hand pressed on my lower back so our crotches touched. I watched couples gliding by behind us, without a single thought, until I felt him under our clothes. I tried to push him away, but his hand pressed me hard so that our crotches rubbed lightly against the fabric of his pants and my skirt. I grew afraid of the calm face that seemed to be plotting the sort of violation I vaguely knew about, right then and there. When the music ended, he dropped my hands and nodded without lifting his eyes. He went away to the other side of the crowd. I returned to my friends, feeling angry and weak.

I jump off the bus after Ting. My legs feel so soft I almost stumble. "What's your rush?" I ask her.

"I can't buy a bikini. My daddy would have a heart attack." Her face is serious.

"Now what shall I tell my parents?" I ask feebly.

"Tell them they were free," she says.

"No, it's a lie."

"Tell them it's a campus fashion."

"No."

She throws down her bags and folds her arms across her chest.

"I have to give them a *reason*. Ah!" I gasp.

"Why, it hurts?" she asks.

"The magazine article you saw—earrings are good for my eyes!" I throw down my bag and hug her. "Thank you, thank you, thank you, Ting."

She pushes me away and scolds, "You nut girl. Come see me. We should go again to get my two-piece."

I pick up my bag and walk into the farmers' market. It's the same messy place, peasants shouting at the top of their lungs about fresh produce. A live hen, her feet bound in tight ropes, hangs upside down on a scale. She flaps her wings and makes the weight slip off. The seller and buyer begin to quarrel over how much she's worth.

"Do you care for eels, little sister? All caught this morning." A woman holds up a fierce-looking eel and I step back.

Her husband is slicing the eels on a wooden board. He picks out a live eel from a basin, knocks its head on the board, then lays its soft body down, holds its head tightly, and stabs a sharp plastic knife into its throat. He slides the knife through its body three times, throws away its guts, bones and head in one piece, pulls its two long slices of flesh through a basin of bloody water, and then puts them away neatly in the pile.

"Only 1.30 yuan a pound," the woman pleads. I shake my head, feeling nauseated at the smell of fresh blood.

I walk swiftly through the market, careful not to touch bloodstained baskets or people, and turn the corner. On the ramp leading to my home, I put down my bags and stretch, wondering if Mom will see me, if she'll run out to greet me.

No one comes out of our apartment building. I waddle down the ramp, my sandals rapping sharply on the cement. How could no one hear me? Maybe Mom isn't home. But her bike is leaning against the sycamore tree. I ring its bell. Inside there's the noise of a chair moving. Then Mom comes out.

She laughs loudly. "My big girl is home. Ha!"

I put down my bags. "Ma."

"Why are you so late? Dad and Wei went looking for you. We thought you were coming at eleven? We waited for you to have lunch." She grabs my arm. "Good girl, you haven't grown thin. How are things?"

"Fine." I smile.

"What is this?" She takes hold of my earring for a closer look. I blush. "They're good for my eyes, you know."

"What?"

"Research says wearing earrings is good for eyesight. You see?"

I take off my glasses, and her face blurs into a white palette. Her eyes fuzz up like two black coals, and I can make out that she isn't smiling.

"Let's go inside." She picks up my bags.

I follow her. In the narrow hallway, I bump into the handlebar of a neighbor's bike. I stifle a groan, put my glasses back on, and make my way inside.

"Did you say you pierced your ears to improve your vision?" she asks when we sit down.

"Basically, yeah."

"Rou!" She pats my cheek. "You young people sure know how to squander money. Your sister went to a summer camp, you know."

My cheeks begin to burn. "Don't you think I look good?"

"Of course my daughter looks good. Hasn't Mom told you before—a nineteen-year-old girl looks her best?" Her eyes sweep from my feet to my face, then freeze at a spot an inch above my head. "They'll come back when they don't find you. Do you want to take a bath now?"

"Yeah." I'm glad to be let off. Obviously Mom isn't going to admire me. Oh well.

I put down the oval wooden bathtub before Mom brings me a half-basin of hot water. I close the windows, pull down the curtain, and lock the door. I take off all my clothes and fill the basin with cold water. Then I kneel and dip my ears into the warm water to rinse off the bloodstain.

I scrub my body inch by inch. The soap slips a few times and bounces around in the tub. I pour the basin of water down my body, pour out the soapy water, and rinse the tub. Then I call Mom for more hot water. I sit and wait until she knocks, then unlock the door and squat down on my heels.

"What did you lock the door for?" she scolds.

I have to stand up to take the basin from her hands. Her eyes pop with such amazement that I'm afraid she might tilt the basin unawares. Her black-coal eyes stare at my naked body as if she is seeing, for the first time, a thing so wondrous and perfect that she, a mother like her, cannot help but admire. Her gaze stuns me so that I can't squat back down fast enough.

"Ma!" I protest.

"Can't I look at my own flesh?" she retorts.

As soon as she leaves, I relock the door. My heart throbs fitfully as if I'm getting the hiccups. Did I read her with my heart or my poor eyes? No one has ever stared at me like that—how could she? Her own flesh. Only she could come up with an excuse like that.

Having rinsed with enough fresh water, I dry myself, put on an old skirt, and comb my hair. I unlock the door and raise my face to the breeze in the hallway.

"Were you embroidering in there, young lady?" Mom shouts at me over the chatter.

Dad and Wei sit straight in their chairs to look at me. I smile at them shyly.

"Well!" Dad says.

Wei says, "Sis."

Mom says, "Now move, let's eat. I sit with my lassie." She pushes Wei over to sit on my left, Dad sits on her right, and she shares the bench with me.

The table is crowded with delicious dishes. Mom grins proudly at my amazement. "It's our first hen this month, very tender. The shrimp was bought specially for you, the fish is very good, and Dad cooked the best eels."

Dad warns Wei, "Remember, Sis is the guest."

Wei puts down his chopsticks. "Sis, please eat," he mumbles with a mouthful of meats.

"I'm eating. Don't mind me. I'm not that hungry."

Wei's chopsticks dive into the eel bowl, and Dad frowns. Mom presses a hand on Dad's wrist.

Dad turns to ask me, "Was your trip okay?"

"Yeah, I came back with Ting, so we loitered a little." Seeing his face become thoughtful, I add, "She has a boyfriend now."

Mom elbows me. "What do you think about Wei?"

"He looks so grown up." Wei chews busily behind closed lips, his dimples round and deep. "And his voice. He sounds almost like Dad now."

Dad cups a hand around his mouth and whispers to me loudly, "Remember the cripple? His sister Lily has an eye on Wei now."

"Shut up!" Wei says. "Sis, don't listen to them. There's no such thing."

Mom and Dad exchange a gleeful glance.

"Are earrings in vogue on campus?" Wei asks.

I hesitate.

"Why hearts?" Mom asks. "They're so. . . ."

"They set off your beautiful complexion," Dad says. "Sis has grown almost prettier than Mom now."

"Sis *is* prettier," Wei says.

"Oh?" Dad is silent for a moment. "What do you say, my old lady?"

"Marvelous!" Mom exclaims. "I can't be prouder! Our children are more beautiful than we!" She kisses me so hard that I wonder if she's made a dimple on my cheek. "Say, are you going with any boy? Now, don't be shy with Mom."

"No," I say uneasily. "What's the rush?"

"You'll give Mom pretty grandchildren?" she presses on.

"They may be ugly." Her eyes pop with horror and I burst out laughing. "Looks don't matter, Ma!"

"But they *do*. They do, for a mother. Your babies will be beautiful."

I'll need to become a mother to see if she guessed right. If I look for my baby's beauty and don't find it, will its beauty find me one day? I cannot yet worry about things like that. For now, I have a nice complexion and a pair of heart earrings that can make me see better—I want to believe.

Wei is laughing. "Babies? Mom, did you say babies?"

Dad clears his throat. "What Mom means is. . . ." He pauses to search for a reason, but that reason doesn't come.

Mom repeats, "Babies, yeah. And you, too, Wei. Cripple's sister is a comely girl."

We all laugh, and Mom is the loudest. Her face is flushed and her wrinkles deepened, and she seems to have more gray hair than I've ever seen.

⚒—What the Father Is Worried About . . .

THE UMBRELLA

A clap of thunder seems to rip open a hole in the sky. I watch rain pelt down in hard sheets from the upstairs balcony and worry about my younger daughter, who is stranded at school. Lian is not a strong kid, and last night she complained about menstrual cramps. I mustn't let her be soaked on her way home and catch her death of cold.

I take out the largest umbrella from storage and dust it off. May has come before I could have our rain gear fixed. Two of its bamboo ribs are broken, so a corner of the oilcloth is drooping. It cannot be folded into a backpack or opened with a flick of a finger. I push it against the wall to slide the runner up the shaft, until it clicks with a squeak. A giant taupe canopy shadows me as I hold up the antique, the only umbrella useful in this downpour. I close it up to put on my raincoat, then hurry away to Lian's school.

Nearing a noodle shop, I catch sight of a tall young man who stands in the doorway holding open his raincoat. The hair on the back of his head is wet and smooth, gleaming jet-black. Passing by him, I become curious about the face the man wears with this fine physique, so I peer back. He bows his head with one cheek pressing on a young woman's temple. There behind the breast of his raincoat hides the little face of my fifteen-year-old daughter.

I whisper, "Lian," and clear my throat.

Lian loosens her grip on the man's waist. With her bangs heaped to one side on her forehead, she appears more surprised than I do. I'm almost too ashamed to speak, but she asks me, "Dad, what're you doing here?"

I thump the ground with my umbrella. "I brought you this, so you wouldn't get drenched." From the corner of my eye I feel the young man watch me.

"Professor Chen," he calls me. I glare at Lian while he explains, "You taught child psychology my sophomore year. I'm from the physical education department. We now practice teaching at Lian's high school—"

I thrust the umbrella into Lian's hands. "Take this and go home!"

Lian sways her hips and faces the young man, who takes her umbrella to open it for her. He pushes the runner up the shaft and locks it with a flick of his wrist. I reach out to warn him not to break more bamboo ribs, only to smooth down the flabby corner of the oilcloth.

"Here you go," he says.

Lian carries the umbrella on her shoulder, rolling the handle a bit while smiling at him. I cannot watch them flirting anymore and pull Lian by the elbow. "Off you go." The young man steps into the rain, but I wave him back. "You don't have to follow us home," I tell him. "Give me your name and phone number. We have to talk."

He gropes in his pants pocket to find an empty cigarette pack, jots down a few lines, and passes it to me. His fingers scald my skin when our hands touch. I raise my head and see he's flushed to the roots of his hair. I walk into the rain and nudge Lian home without another word.

Lian drags her heeled slippers noisily into the living room. Her half-wet bangs are combed out neatly, as if dabbled with mousse. She plops down on the sofa and crosses her legs, letting her red-dotted pajama pants climb up her ankles.

"He was taking me home because he wore a raincoat, and I didn't have an umbrella." She eyes her mother for support. "Then it started to pour and we had to find shelter."

"Shelter? You call being in his arms shelter?" The words fly out of my mouth before I can think. My wife squeezes my wrist, but I pull away. I'm not wrong. Lian is the one who's making a mistake by lying to her father.

Her eyelids droop. "Leave me alone."

"Lian, I wouldn't tell you this if it wasn't true." I fumble in my pocket for a cigarette before I recall I quit more than a decade ago. "You're not only our youngest, but also the brightest. You can have it all—career, love, and family. Do you really want to throw away everything to mess with your PE teacher?"

She bites her lower lip to conceal a smile. "His name is Kai Shi, and he was only taking me home."

I tell her in the softest tone I can manage, "Lian, I saw what I saw."

She leaps up from the sofa and knocks off a doily. "There wasn't much space under the roof, and we stood close. So what?" Standing with her arms akimbo, she looks like a spring manne-quin in a shop window. "Now if you'll excuse me, I have to do my homework." The door of her room bangs closed.

My wife pats my hand. "Good try, old man." She stoops to pick up the doily and smoothes it out on the arm of the sofa.

I stride to the balcony to watch the rain, and spare her the news that I'm going to smoke again.

I fasten the top button of my black tunic suit as I stroll toward the playground. I want to look a bit severe to my former stu-dent Kai, who is teaching his class to throw the javelin. Kai, in his parrot-green sportswear, holds the shaft on a cord grip at ear level, runs seven steps, then halts suddenly to hurl the jav-elin overhand and send it soaring through air. It lands in the sparse grass with its point striking the field, its upturned tail trembling in the breeze.

I cough loudly in order to drown out the boys' murmuring. Kai sees me and nods slightly. "You're going to practice like I demonstrated." He lines the boys up. "One person at a time, and play safe." He waits for a boy to toss a javelin that drops flatly to the ground, then walks toward me with his hands in his pockets.

"Professor Chen, I didn't get your call."

"I came to take my daughter home and thought to make a quick stop here." He avoids my eyes, while I swing my umbrella like a heavy cane. "You know it's against school regulations for you to pursue a student, don't you? You can get disciplinary treatment for this, which will reflect badly on your résumé."

"We aren't dating." He scrapes sand with the spikes under his sole and marks parallel bruises on the ground. "Besides, she isn't my student. I teach the boys' team."

"How old are you?"

"Twenty-three."

I take out a pack of Marlboros to offer him a cigarette, but he pushes my hand away. So I tap the cigarette on the carton, then put it into my own mouth. "Can you tell me what I taught you in the child psychology class?" I strike a match.

"Child psychology?"

"Yeah." The smoke burns my throat, so I breathe slowly. The cigarette that used to relax me makes me nervous.

"Oh, boy." He paces a few steps with his hands on his hips. "I remember in the last class, you said it's beneficial to raise a girl like a half-boy so she'll grow up to be more assertive."

"And?"

"Vice versa, to raise a boy like a half-girl so he'll become an empathetic person."

I feel more impressed than I would like to, and stub out my cigarette. "I didn't teach you to take advantage of your students, did I? Lian is only fifteen." I step forward. "She ought to go to a university and meet some boy her own age." We stand so close I can smell a warm body scent and sickly sweet aftershave emanating from him. "I want a promise from you—will you stay away from her?"

He folds his arms across his chest, with a confident smile of someone who enjoys his strong body and pretty face. "I already told you we weren't dating."

"But will you promise me?"

"Promise you what? Never do what I haven't done?" He shakes his head. "Excuse me, I have to get back to my class now."

Kai blows his whistle to warn a boy, who whips the knees of the boy behind him with the tail of his javelin. "Put that down!" he shouts. "I didn't give you permission to punch holes in someone else's leg. . . ."

I have to walk away before more words fall on my sensitive ears.

Lian doesn't seem to notice me when our eyes meet. I wave at her again with my umbrella before she leaves her girlfriend to skip over to my side.

"Dad, it's not raining!"

I look up at the cloudy sky. "You're right. For some reason I rushed off to have our umbrella fixed."

She giggles and thrusts her arm into mine. "I got you to worry, didn't I?"

I tug her arm to feel its soft weight. Wearing heeled pumps, she stands almost taller than I, but she's light, shy of fifty kilos. I wonder if I might worry about her less if she were a little stronger. She's grown twelve centimeters in her post–high jump years but has put on little weight. Peddlers gaze at us as we pass by their storefronts. Suddenly I feel proud of having my winsome daughter hanging on my arm and walking home with me.

She leans her head on my shoulder. "Dad, do you really think I'm smarter than my older sister?"

I pat the back of her hand. "You also have to see that she works harder than you, and she's a very serious-minded girl."

She peers at the noodle shop where I found her yesterday, with her mouth half open. "Oh."

"She was a straight-A student, and so are you, of course. But she never wasted her time messing around. Instead, she studied English in her spare time and got into a U.S. college with a full scholarship. You should learn from her and adopt a long-term plan to secure a good future. As the old saying goes, she who throws a long line catches a big fish."

Lian twists her body to pull her arm away. I touch her sleeve but don't dare to grab hold of her. She's a big girl now. Since her siblings have gone away, I have to admit I've been stricter with her than with my two older children. I can never admit to anyone that Lian is my favorite, though it seems right for me to make up for all my previous failings as a father while I still have a chance. She leaps ahead of me in a deer-like trot, her long hair flying behind her. I hope she hasn't become an object of pursuit for young men—it's too soon. She's a mere child in an adult's height. My worries are already a nuisance to her, and she prevents me from being overly protective. If she does care for him, she'll find ways to outwit me and consummate the love affair. Rather than rebelling against me, it'll be better if she learns a trick or two before she takes to proper courting.

"Fishing?" Lian asks and puffs out her cheeks like a goldfish. "Who can see *me* carrying a rod standing on the riverbank?"

"A hand line," I correct her, "is what we're going to use." From behind the door I take out the new cane pole, at the tip of which hangs an eyed hook on the end of a nylon line.

"Angling is a sport for young and old alike, so you mustn't have prejudice against it."

"I'm not prejudiced." She runs her finger and thumb down the line to pinch the hook. "I just don't have the patience for it."

"Don't sell yourself short, Daughter." I cast my line across the room to hook a doily on the arm of the sofa, when my wife enters the room.

"Aren't you forgetting yourself, old man?" she scolds and unhooks the doily.

Lian and I burst into laughter.

"I haven't fished ever since I became a dad. But, you see, it's like riding a bike. You never forget the basics."

"Fishing basics?" My wife chuckles.

I wink at her, and she falls silent. She knows I plan to spend time with Lian outdoors, not only for the sport's sake.

"In order to catch a fish, you have to use your hands and arms, as well as your brain." I pat my head. "It is a battle of wits between a fish and an angler, similar to any mind game between two people."

My wife sits on the sofa.

"A lot of girls say they don't care for fishing," I tell them. "But in the village where I grew up, quite a few girls caught bigger fish than the boys did. Can you guess why?"

"They're more patient?" Lian shrugs. "Not me, Dad."

"When it comes to fishing, a boy is just as patient, until a big fish bites. Then he gets so excited that he starts fighting rough." I pick up the hook and a little line to stretch them out before her eyes. "You see, the line may be strong enough, but a fish mouth isn't, so the hook will pull out. A girl who can reel in with a gentle hand isn't so likely to lose her catch."

My wife gives me the thumbs-up.

Lian takes my pole to lay it flat on her lap, then plants it on the ground to see how tall it stands.

My wife raises the hand line onto Lian's shoulder and strokes her hair. "Finish your homework early, so you can go fishing with Dad on Sunday."

Lian turns her head to watch the hook dangle behind her back.

The wispy branches of a weeping willow brush the pond surface, half covered with lily pads and duckweed. My galoshes sink into mud that smells of grass root marinated with lake water.

"Don't stomp on the bank." I hush Lian beside me. "You're scaring away the fish."

She leaps up. "Where, where're the fish?"

I pull her behind the stump of a fallen willow. "We're going to split up," I tell her. "I'd like to settle here for a little bit."

Lian points her finger at the lake. "Look!" A red carp hops out of the lily pads and rolls in the air. "The carp jumped!" She claps her hands.

"What're you doing?" I drag her twenty meters away from the pond to lecture her. "Don't talk so loud. Fish can hear us. You already spooked the prize carp in the pond. Can you keep quiet so we don't go home empty-handed?" She nods and sticks out her tongue. "One other thing, you shouldn't stand so close to me, because when I pick a spot, I mark my territory."

She blows the bangs off her forehead. "Dad, I thought you were going to teach me how to fish."

"What do you think I just did?" I pat her shoulder. "Come on, you go first."

She tiptoes to the stump and peers back at me for my approval. I nod at her and watch her drop the line in the water. For a beginner like her, one spot is as good as the other, since she has to rely on her luck to lure the fish to bite. All I want is peace between us when she stays away from Kai.

Carp like to dig up plants and nibble on their roots, stirring up the bottom silt. I pace the bank to find clouds of mud with bubbles erupting on the surface, then squat down to cast my line. Beneath the green, weedy water, I imagine my fish soup simmering in the pond, which is shaped like a giant caldron.

I watch my bobber dance up and down on the water surface. A fish has been nibbling the bait for a while and finally pulls the bobber under, when I strike! The line rips out of the water without the hook at the end.

"Darn it!" I mutter under my breath, and stoop to comb the grass for the missing hook.

Lian studies my face as I walk toward her, ignoring her hand line as it sinks under the weeds. I cup my hands around my mouth to shout to her, "Strike! The fish is biting!" She lifts the pole to fling it back. Nothing. Luckily, the hook remains on the end of the line.

"It took the bait." She scrapes off the sticky paste to put on a new dough ball.

"Make sure the tip of your hook doesn't show." I squeeze her dough ball into a narrow strip. "A carp is a very cunning fish. It likes to mouth a piece of food a dozen times, spitting it out each time, before it makes up its mind to swallow it."

She rubs her hand and forearm. "My wrist is sore."

I feel the heat of sunshine in my hair. It's a perfect day for carp and other bottom dwellers to sunbathe in the shallow water. "You can either continue to fish or carry the umbrella over both our heads. Your mom will snap at me if I let you get sunburned."

She squints at me. "What're you doing here, Dad?"

"I lost my hook." I ignore her gleeful titter. "Next time I'll remember to bring a couple of spares."

She picks up the handle of the oilcloth umbrella. "Until then, Dad, open the canopy for us."

The sun is going down behind the woods on the other side of the riverbank and making the water shimmer like brittle glass. The chattering of magpies rattles the air, while paired swallows glide across the pond to catch dragonflies. Perhaps they're busy feeding their young.

Lian whips her pole back through the slender willow leaves, with a silver fish wagging its tail at the end of her line. "I caught a fish!" she squeals. "I caught it!"

I'm afraid of ripping the grass carp's jaw as I try to take out the hook. Then I put my finger on its bloody mouth. "This will calm a carp down, even after a brutal fight."

"We're going to have fish soup tonight!" She leaps up and down as if she had springs under her soles.

I pinch its limp body to drop it in the pail. "It's too tiny and bony." I wipe my slimy fingers on the grass, stand up to close the umbrella and gather our tackle. "You may have an easier time if Mom pan-fries it."

"The soup will be a little thin, but each of us will have a sip." She dumps the remaining dough balls into the river and coos, "Hurry up and feed, fish, while you still can!"

I watch her cup her hands together, scoop up river water into the pail, and throw in a piece of duckweed. "Who's gotten hooked here, you or the carp?" I ask.

She slides the hand line onto her shoulder. "We're coming back next Sunday, right, Dad?"

I pat her on the head. "You're a fast learner, obliging me to do it with a sip of your fish soup."

She giggles. "Bribe accepted."

We then march home, two victorious anglers.

Next Sunday is cloudy, so I prepare extra line and hooks for our fishing trip.

"Grass carp will be hiding at the bottom of the river today," I tell Lian. "We ought to throw a long line to catch a big fish."

"Enough bluffing already." My wife hands me the oilcloth umbrella. "You two bring me that red carp home tonight, all right?"

"You bet, Mom." Lian elbows me.

As soon as we're outside, I feel a cool raindrop on my brow. Trotting ahead of me, Lian ascends the ramp and sways her narrow hips a bit. She's been talking about carp the whole week, so I don't mention the rain and dampen her spirit. We remain silent until we reach the lake. I glimpse a tall figure standing by the willow stump where we fished last week. Facing away from us, he wears a raincoat and brimmed hat.

I stop to tell Lian, "Looks like our spot is taken."

"I'll go elsewhere," Lian says.

The man turns his face, and Lian waves at him. It's Kai Shi, the PE teacher. If he's here to ruin our good time, I won't let him. Our eyes meet briefly, before I pull away to watch Lian drop her line in the water. Then I drag myself to address Kai.

"How's your catch?" I whisper.

He points at the pail on the ground. "Carp and such."

His rod is balanced perfectly in the strong hand with which he threw the javelin across three-quarters of the playground.

"How did you find this place?" I ask him in a strained low voice.

"I've been fishing here for four years. It's the first time I've seen you two." He glances at me. "It's real nice in summer. I met my girlfriend here."

"Oh." I try not to raise my voice. "You have a girlfriend."

"Had." He rips the line from the water to lean the rod against the tree. "Do you care for a cigarette?"

"Okay." I take his Peony, sniff it, then put it in my mouth.

He strikes a match to light both our cigarettes. "It may be my last time to fish here. I've found a job in my hometown. I will leave as soon as I get my diploma."

I peer at Lian to see if she might have overheard us. She stands erect and stares at the bobber. Her lips are pouting, and she has a slight double chin. I take a long pull on my cigarette, feeling heated tobacco smoke fill my lungs.

"I should apologize to you then." I rack my brain for the polite words. "For having so rashly accused you of pursuing my daughter."

"It's not your fault." He blows some broken rings. "I was feeling awfully lonely when I first met Lian, and she was always giggling. I admit I wished for a piece of her light heart. It's immoral because I am her teacher."

I stub out my Peony and wipe my mouth. Words cannot describe how glad I am he's going away.

"I take her fishing because it gives her something to do with her hands," I finally tell him.

"It's a good hobby." He picks up the rod to return to fishing.

Light drizzle needles the smooth surface of the water. I stare at my bobber and wonder if I need an extra sinker to anchor my hook more steadily, when the water splashes as if someone has dived into the pond. Kai pulls his rod vertical and fiercely reels in his line. The noise drowns out my murmur "Gently."

He yells, "Come on, boy," and sways from side to side to keep up with the quick darting run at the end of his line, which gets tangled up with some lily pads.

A moment later he reels in the rest of his line along with the empty hook.

"Did you see that carp?" he shouts. "It must've been five kilos!"

Lian drops her hand line. I follow her to go over and check Kai's hook. It's sharp and bloodless.

"You should've fought it a little gentler," I tell him. "Its mouth can't take your full wrist strength."

"I can't help it." He flexes his hands. "A carp fight makes my blood boil."

Lian pinches the hook and pulls the line with her thumb and finger. "Is it a red carp?" she asks with a blush.

"No, it's silver." Kai fixes his eyes on her. "Why, are you after a red one?" She nods with a grin. "Tell you what, I'll let you try my rod and see if you can do better with a reel." He squats down to teach her reeling. "When you get a strike, just reel it in, and don't give it any slack!"

"Do it gently," I add. "Does your line reach the lake bottom?"

"Not quite. It's carp-spawning season, so they're feeding everywhere and come to the shallows all the time." He baits the hook for Lian. "Honey-scented dough ball is a carp's favorite. I bet your dad didn't give you that." He stands up and dusts his hands. "You all set? I'm going to take a break."

I wait for Lian to settle in, then follow Kai to the top of the bank, where he sits in the wet grass. I pass him a pack of Marlboros, from which he picks out a cigarette. The drizzle has grown denser, and I light our cigarettes after a few attempts.

"Carp are feeding and spawning in this rain." He flicks off the ash. "What an exciting day for fishing!" He can hardly suppress a smile. How young he looks with his bushy eyebrows and smooth forehead!

"So, did you find a satisfactory job?" I eye my umbrella lying in the grass down the bank.

"A high school with a pilot program for physical education." He rubs his soles on the grass and bends his knees to fold his long legs in front of his chest. "My ex-girlfriend wanted me to teach at the community college here, which has PE classes only as an elective, but I want to be a real teacher, you know, a leader of a group of children."

I gaze at Lian, who stands holding the rod and seems blissfully forgetful of the young man who lent it to her. She's still a child, and will be for a while longer. Thank goodness.

"It's sort of like being a parent."

Before I know it, my hand reaches out to pat his knee. Then I look into his eyes for the first time, taking in his black irises and clear, spotless whites.

"I'll remember that, Professor Chen." His long lashes tremble when a raindrop splatters on his cheek.

"Excuse me, I have to go back to my daughter, or she'll get wet."

Kai nods at me with a boyish smile.

I walk quietly toward Lian. When she turns to me and presses a finger on her mouth, I stretch out my arm to bring the umbrella over her head.

I notice the rod slanting in Lian's hand. She stumbles forward, out from under my umbrella. The duckweeds have swallowed her bobbers. I grab hold of her rod and shout, "Strike!"

"I know." Lian reels in the line while being pulled left and right.

Kai runs to our help and yells, "Jerk your rod to hook it up!" Lian flicks her wrist. "Don't give it any slack!" Kai grips the rod to keep it steady and vertical. The fish, now in the shallow, thrashes about the lily pads and sprays a wave of white water.

"Dad, it's pulling me down," Lian screams.

"It's okay. You keep reeling and let us take care of the rod."

Kai's and my hands hold the rod firmly back, while Lian continues to reel.

Just before the fish is lifted off the water, Kai says, "Now flip it over," and yanks the rod, and we swing the fish onshore. The hook pulls out of the fish's mouth in midair. Lian skips over to press the writhing carp against the wet grass, and puts her finger on its mouth until it quiets down. Its silver scales glisten like armor.

"I thought I was getting pulled under." Lian peers up at us, panting.

"This boy weighs about three kilos." Kai crouches down to have a closer look. "A healthy carp rockets off like a torpedo."

Thunder breaks out in the near distance. I pick up the umbrella to hold it above our heads.

"The carp will be enough for the four of us." Lian's eyes are bright and happy as if brimming over with rainwater. "Can Mr. Shi come have dinner with us, Dad?"

At least my daughter knows how to thank her helper.

"Let's hurry." I lift my umbrella higher when Kai stands up. "Off to home we go."

"It's okay, Professor Chen. I'm wearing my raincoat." He steps aside to let Lian take the space next to me. "Believe it or not, it's the first time I've helped to catch a fish big enough to feed a family."

"I believe you." I pat his wet sleeve. "And you'll appreciate it even more when you taste it."

Lian carries the pail and swings it a bit, while we gather our tackle. "We threw a short line and caught a big fish, didn't we, Dad?"

"Not without Mr. Shi's help."

"Of course."

"It takes a kinder person to lend you a rod than give you a fish." Kai walks ahead, so I'm not sure if he's heard us. "As the old saying goes, a teacher for a day is a father for a lifetime," I tell Lian loudly.

Kai waves his hand with his back to us, and Lian smiles. Just before crossing the road, he reaches out to the willow branches and runs his fingers through them as if combing soft green hair.

THE WOMEN IN LOVE

姊—What the Older Daughter Has Got . . .

DREAM LOVER

When my boyfriend Sammy asks me to move in with him, I tell him I'm not ready. Living together is a semi-marriage; I don't feel up to it yet.

"You are not ready!" Sammy wraps the bed sheet around me and holds my half-covered body in his arms. "Why not, Rou?"

I giggle. We haven't played like this for a long while. Now that my contract with Fidelity has ended, I don't have to work on the weekend. Even better, since I have my green card, I'm free to shop for a new contract that may take me outside of Boston, anywhere in the country.

He tightens his grip on my waist and repeats, "Why not?" His nose is almost touching mine. He has a long, very straight nose for a Chinese man, which I take to be a look of decency.

I stamp a light kiss on his straight nose, then try to push him away. "You're choking me!" I yell. I don't worry that my neighbors, whom I hardly know, may overhear me through the thin wall. Besides, my lease has just ended.

He loosens his clutch and I kick off the bed sheet. I like to press my naked body on him after we make love—it makes me feel safe and needed. But Sammy wants to cover me up while we talk about serious subjects, so he won't be too distracted by my body, he once told me.

"You don't get shy before me anymore," he says and lets me wrap my leg around him.

I pause, suppressing the urge to take back my leg. Then I pull up the bed sheet to cover myself a bit. I smile at him shyly while he runs his fingers through my long hair. Three years ago, when I met him at Boston University, I had short hair. He was only a year older than I, but had come to the U.S. two years before I did. He had the finesse to court me for a short week, before he tackled me. I was at once relieved and resentful of him for taking my virginity. Of all the men on the face of the earth, why him? I had saved myself for twenty years. Why should one week of romance put an end to my girlhood? But I didn't want him to fall out of love with me. So I began my routines with birth control pills and Victoria's Secret, and I grew my hair long to please him.

"I can't live without you, Rou. Move in with me." As he swings his leg over me, I wrap my leg around his waist.

"Yes, you can," I reply. "What about before you met me? How about your ex in New Hampshire?" I see the hurt in his eyes and kiss him. "Oh, please don't go back to her, I beg you." I am Sammy's second girlfriend and may not be the last.

He hugs me tightly. "No," he says. "Never. Don't you worry."

I sigh with relief. After all, I'm going to take a three-week vacation to visit my family in Nanjing. I don't want to go by myself but Sammy has to work. He said he can never go back to China now, since he has to watch football, baseball, basketball, and hockey all year long and cheer for the New England teams. Because I haven't gone back in five years, I want to visit China before I lose touch with a special old friend of mine.

"Seriously," he says. "You decide when you come back if you want to live with me. But for this month, you can move your stuff into my living room and save seven hundred dollars to compensate for your traveling expenses. Not to mention, you'll be doing some summer tourists a favor by giving them a downtown studio."

"But I have so many things," I say.

There're the queen-sized bed where we're lying, a full-sized dresser, mirror, desk, chairs, bookcase, books, computer, printer, TV, VCR, TV stand, my kitchen stuff, bathroom stuff, and clothes. Oh, and the file cabinet, where I've saved all my mail, along with the copies of my own letters, for the past five years.

"Honey, we can manage," he says.

He's right. He has only a sofa bed and a dining table in his one-bedroom apartment. We always eat at his place, then come back to sleep in my bed. We've made love in his hard crooked sofa bed only a handful of times. But, being near my apartment, the sofa bed is convenient. I can throw him out after we fight about some trifles. Sammy tells me it's not a copout for me to settle for my first boyfriend. We've had our bumpy times, which he calls breakups, and by working through them, our relationship is renewed. Still, I flirted with other men when we had our fallings-out. Sammy always waited for me to come back to him, and every time I did.

The next day I write my friend Xu in China a postcard about my return. "Dear Xu Liang," I begin. Then I recall he has been married for two years while I haven't written him at all. I white-out the "Dear" and replace it with "Mr." and then go on, "I hope you're doing well. I'd like to let you know I'm going home for a three-week vacation from 6/1–6/21. My number in Nanjing is 579–9865. Let's catch up, if you're in the area." I sign my name.

I search my old mail for his address and find copies of my own letters that make me blush. "You were the first man I thought I could love," I wrote soon after I came to the U.S. I was so lonely then that I wrote to my family and friends all the time. After I began dating Sammy, I gradually stopped writing and earned enough money to call home every month. When Xu was getting married two and a half years ago, I wrote to him, "Married or not I will always cherish you," and "*Right Here Waiting* is the theme song of my devotion," etc. I wrote those last two letters on nights when Sammy was home sleeping on his sofa bed.

In the afternoon Sammy helps me move my things. He almost slips while we carry the locked file cabinet upstairs.

"What do you have in here?" he asks. "Can you take some stuff out?"

"Honey, let's just move it, all right?" I plead.

He lifts the heavy cabinet on his shoulder. I back slowly up the stairs and feel grateful that he doesn't insist on unlocking it. We push the file cabinet into his walk-in closet, and I slide the key into my packed suitcase.

At night Sammy is too tired to make love. I lie beside him wide awake, while the old letters I read during the day all come back to me. I never told Sammy that I had an ex, too, in my own way. Xu once was, still is, and will always be my dream lover.

I must have been a pitiful sight to him at the 1988 freshman orientation at Shanghai University. I was eighteen. It was late summer, when jean shorts were popular among girls who had shapely legs. I was trim enough for such a display, but I had never worn anything higher than my knees, nor had I ever wanted to. Maybe my seersucker trousers and cotton shoes gave away that I was new in town, for he came up to greet me.

"Where're you from, miss?"

No one called me "miss" back home. I whispered, "Nanjing," already blushing.

He smiled, a suave and confident smile. "Welcome. My name is Xu Liang. I am a senior, from Wenzhou." He was thin, of medium-height, and large-eyed like a typical southerner, though he was pale-skinned and very handsome.

He gave me a business card and said, "Stop in to our poetry club and have a chat with us sometime." He turned to greet other freshmen, while I read the beige gilt card, which included his long list of titles, from managing editor of the school newspaper to president of the Poets' Corner. He had forgotten to ask my name, but I liked being called "miss"—it felt genteel.

During my second semester, I finished my TOEFL exam and started to attend Xu's poetry club meetings. I had no ear for rhymes, but I loved spying on him at the center of a talkative crowd. I imagined that he could get a fine girlfriend, with his face, his voice, his smile, not to mention his style—he was a beautiful dancer. I also had a weakness for the snacks served at the meeting (Xu had a small budget from the school): spiced sunflower seeds, preserved beef jerky, and bean paste moon cakes. Every week I looked forward to something better and was never disappointed.

I attended the weekly readings for four months without being noticed, until I was the only girl left in the club. One day Xu asked why I hadn't read anything.

"I can't write poetry," I said.

It was the first week of May, and he had just gotten an increased budget. He brought in two giant bags of M&Ms that I couldn't take my eyes off. Imported M&Ms were shockingly expensive back then. My mouth watered when I read the bag: "Melt in Your Mouth, But Not in Your Hands." I imagined that they must be even better than milk chocolate, which I loved, but which only came in brown and white chunks.

He caught me gawking at the M&Ms. "Promise you'll read something next time, or you can't have these."

I licked my lips and scanned the room. Nine pairs of eyes were fixed upon my face. I peered at him and said nothing.

"You just came for the food." He broke into a laugh. "Now open your hands." He ripped the bag open and poured me a great heap.

It was not true that I just went for the food, though if I couldn't attract him, I would settle for the candies. I savored my chocolate, letting each M&M melt slowly in my mouth and sweeten my tongue from tip to root. I was a little disappointed to find a yellow M&M melted in my palm, revealing its brown inside. I pressed the piece into my mouth and licked my palm, wrapped up seven candies in my handkerchief for the next day (red, orange, yellow, green, blue, brown, purple— enough colors to make a rainbow), then wiped my wet palm on my brown polyester pants. I had very sweaty hands; maybe some people, like Xu, had the right kind of hands that wouldn't melt the chocolate. I peered up at him and saw he was watching me rub my hand on my thigh. Suddenly I became worried: did my slacks make my legs look bulky?

Sammy turns to my side and throws his arm around me. The temperature tonight in Boston is still in the fifties. I put his arm under the sheet and pull the quilt over his back. His hand moves down to my thigh and strokes me a few times, while I giggle quietly. Listening to his even breathing, I wonder whether the fits I throw around him sometimes are the result of his falling short of my dream of a lover. What was it that made my heart stop whenever Xu looked in my direction? I yawn, wishing Sammy could've stayed up with me on the last night before my long trip back to China.

I wake up in the room where I grew up and find Sammy isn't sleeping beside me. I'm lying alone on a sandy-colored bamboo mat, under a pink throw and enclosed in a white gauze mosquito net. Feeling sweat on my greasy face, I get out of the net to sit by the open windows. The balcony of the opposite building is less than ten meters away. Some underwear, tee shirts, tank tops, and a miniskirt are flapping in the warm breeze like tied kites. Through the green screen windows, the slice of sky is a drowsy white.

"Did you sleep well?" Mom asks when I enter the bathroom.

"Sort of." I yawn, rubbing the slim marks of bamboo mat on my right cheek.

I feel as if I've been home for more than a month, but it is only the end of my second week. I must've lost some weight, and my hair has grown longer. I should've cut off my long hair before I came to stay in this heat. How can I indulge in my femininity when I don't have enough hot water to wash it thoroughly?

In the shower, I rub a small blob of shampoo into my hair and rinse frantically. Home life has been a disappointment so far. I showed pictures of Sammy to my family.

"*My boyfriend,*" I said.

Mom said, "Why, he is scrawny-looking."

I said, "Mom, he's *my man.*"

My parents just looked at me warily, and my sister smiled. Nobody grilled me about how I was his woman; they all wanted me to save face, pretend that I'm still a virgin. I haven't heard a word from Xu—maybe he is too busy with his married life to bother with me. The shampoo flows into my eyes and stings out a few tears.

I hear a knock on the door. "Yeah?" I shout.

The door is opened, and Mom comes in to give me the cordless phone. "For you."

I turn off the water. "Hello?" I say in English.

"Well, now you speak like an American miss," a man's voice says in Chinese.

"Huh?"

"This is Xu Liang. How are you, Rou?"

"Oh, Xu, did you get my postcard?" I slide down the soapy tub to prop my arms on the edge.

"Sure did," he says. "I just came back from Beijing on a business trip. Do you want to come out here for a few days? I can arrange the airfare. You'll be doing me a favor by using up my piles of frequent-flyer mileage."

"To where? Are you in town?" I ask.

"To my home, Wenzhou, in the Yandang Mountains," he says. "How did you become so dense after living in the States for a couple of years?"

I peer at my naked body and stretch out my legs. He's so bossy, but I like it. "I haven't been myself lately. Being cooped up at home doesn't help me a bit, you know."

He laughs, and his voice makes me feel weak. My God, that is *him*. I wonder if he can picture me lying naked in the tub talking to him.

"Yes or no?" he asks.

"I'll ask Mom, but I think it's a yes."

"Good. I'll book you a ticket from the 15th to the 17th. How's that?"

"Sounds great. Thank you so much." I wipe my forehead and more tears flow, even without shampoo in my eyes.

"I'll call you back about your flights. See ya."

I hang up and put the phone down on the floor. Turning the shower back on, I rinse myself until the hot water is gone and the cold water splashes me numb. My hands are shaking and my legs unsteady when I dry myself. I run a sandalwood comb through my wet hair, then peer over my shoulder at my backside. My hand reaches for the doorknob before I realize I'm still naked. I sigh, slap my cheeks to calm myself, then put on my clothes, check myself in the mirror, and recomb my hair.

I sit down at the breakfast table. "I'm going to visit some friends in Wenzhou, Ma."

She has put out chicken feet, frog legs, pigeon eggs, and bowls of other delicacies that I cannot name.

"Who?" she asks.

"Xu called. He sent me an airline ticket for tomorrow."

"Who's Xu?" Mom asks.

"A college friend." My face warms up. I don't want Mom to see me blush, so I rush into the bathroom.

This is not funny. Although I haven't seen Xu in five years, speaking of him makes me feel like I'm still eighteen years old.

"Mom, it's sweet of him to invite me to the Yandang Mountains." I splash water onto my face, then wipe it dry on the towel. "He doesn't have to." I return to the table. "Oh, I wish it weren't so hot." I cup my cheeks in my hands.

"It will be cooler in the mountains," Mom says. "You know Nanjing is one of the Three Furnaces of China. The Yandang Mountains are heavenly in the summer. You have to be very careful in Wenzhou, pickpockets abound, and everything is so overpriced. Mom hasn't gone back in ten years, but I can tell you, a few years doesn't change an old town—"

"I'll be careful." I jab my chopsticks into a pigeon egg and douse it with hot sauce. I can eat it when it doesn't taste like an unhatched bird.

Flying in the white clouds, I cannot see the green mountain valley thousands of feet below, where Xu's home is. I wonder where I buried my love for him in these two years, and if our reunion is a sign and an opportunity for us to finally consummate our romance. Perhaps he knows I cannot return in vain. After the Tiananmen Square protests in 1989, I left China so hastily that we didn't even say goodbye.

I didn't know that day would be my last time attending the poetry meeting. I arrived early, ready to shine as the only female moderator in the club. My heart leapt out to him when he opened the door of the stuffy room, but I was afraid of looking at him.

"Did I miss anyone? Is anyone else going to read?" I shrilled like a little girl.

"How about you?" He put down two bags of Hershey's Kisses. They must have cost a fortune!

I stared at the silvery Kisses and felt very silly. I had totally forgotten about the business of writing poetry.

He tore open the bag and poured a heap on my notepad. "Enjoy." He met my eyes and added, "Brother." I heard some scattered chuckles.

I was wearing my pink polyester dress that made me feel itchy but pretty, a pink satin ribbon tying up my newly permed hair. His calling me "Brother" made me turn so red that my back itched against the polyester. I reached out to pull the suffocating fabric off my sweating skin and sighed more loudly than I had wanted to.

Xu sat down in the chair opposite me, looking toward me but not at me. I turned back and saw our 1989 school calendar taped on the wall. In the second week of May, the pro-democracy protests were revving up. It didn't seem to be dangerous, not yet. We sat around and chewed our Kisses, safe in each other's company. None of us knew who would soon get lucky and who would be whipped. Three months later, Xu, the brilliant poet, was fired from the school paper and graduated to become a realtor who ran his own company, while I obtained my student visa to the U.S.

It's early morning on the other side of the earth: who is Sammy lying with? It seems easy for him to call his ex in New Hampshire to have a chat, who is in the same time zone with him. Sammy told me nothing about her except that she wasn't a virgin. I wonder if she was prettier or sexier than I. Sammy must've compared us as lovers—was it a sacrifice for him to choose me? I've had no one else in my life besides Xu, who doesn't really count, at least not yet.

In the light of a brilliant full moon, the plane is descending. Below, houses emerge out of darkening clouds. I can't believe that after five long years I'm really here. Does my hair look neat? I sit numbly, unable to thumb through my purse for a mirror. What should I say to him?

Outside the terminal, people shout in a dialect I don't understand. I glance around anxiously, thinking what a laughing-stock I'll be if he does not show. Then I see a young man wave at me and recognize him. He grins at me, wearing a striped polo shirt and smart haircut, looking so strange yet familiar. His face has become rounder, his eyes smaller, and he's even paler than I remembered. When he walks closer, I smell his cologne, the same kind Sammy uses.

"I was worried," I stutter. "What if you didn't come?"

"Why?" He smiles. "Impossible."

He takes my bag and walks me to his chauffeured car. I slide into the back seat. He puts the bag on the seat next to me and closes my door. Then he gets into the front and talks to the driver, a stout young man, in the local dialect.

"We're going to the city of Wenzhou," he says in Mandarin and I nod.

"It's so much cooler here—Nanjing is like a furnace." There are a pair of toy flags by the passenger side mirror, one Chinese and the other American. "Nice car. You must be doing well for yourself."

He nods slightly. "I'm thinking of buying a new car, probably a Cadillac."

"What's this?" I ask.

"It's an Audi. I'm going to take a road test next week. I wish you could have come a week later when I'll have my license."

I sigh. "I can't drive a stick shift."

He peers at me. "Seriously?"

"Yeah. I can't even parallel park."

"Do you have your driver's license?"

I hand it to him. "I have Visa Gold, too."

"Nice." He gives me back the card. "Wenzhou is very strict about drivers' licenses, and I don't have time to go to the driving school."

I nod and say, "I wish I could teach you." In the dark, I begin to blush.

"We'll see to that," he murmurs.

The pedestrians are almost touching our car. I don't dare to drive in such crowded streets.

"You probably never have to put up with bureaucracy like in Wenzhou." He raises his voice. "But don't get me wrong, I love my hometown, and I love China. Patriotism is almost back in fashion now. I have a number of graduated friends who wrote to me asking about job opportunities."

I watch a cute couple in matching white suits from the rear window, until they are out of sight. We come to a quiet street.

"Do you want to try your hand at driving?" Xu asks.

"Sure," I say.

The chauffeur steps out of the car to let me take the driver's seat.

I pull the stick shift and step on the gas. The car stops, and we lean forward. I start the car again and repeat my failure. I look down in my lap and see the blurry white of my thighs at the torn end of my jean shorts.

"So that's it." Xu removes his gaze from my legs. "We can't spare Jin even for a couple of days."

When the chauffeur returns, Xu hands him a cigarette and explains something. Jin glances at me. In the shadow, Xu's face looks inconsolable.

Xu and Jin pick me up from the hotel the next day to head for the mountains. The Yandang Mountains, Mom told me, are famous for their feng shui and high geomantic quality, and Wenzhou people are very superstitious. There's a grove of tombstones on the face of the mountains, flaunting the wealth of the dead. One of those opulent tombs is my great-grandfather's, who had three wives. As far as I know, only one wife was buried with him.

"Mountain of tombs," I say with a sigh.

"There're a lot of wealthy people here; millionaires, even billionaires, aren't so rare as they were a few years ago," Xu tells me.

"Are there poor people in this town?" I ask.

"Me!" He chuckles. "I'm sure there are, but they don't stand out like rich people do. It's impossible to get around in this town if you're poor. You see, we have to pay toll for every quarter of a kilometer." He peers at the camera hanging down from my neck. "And taking pictures costs extra at a scenic spot."

I hold my camera. "I won't bother, then."

He fixes his eyes on my chest, as if he doesn't believe what I said. I try to smile, and he says, "You didn't hang up your phone last night."

"My phone? I only made a wakeup call." No wonder it didn't ring this morning!

Xu mutters under his breath, "It was busy all night."

He looks straight ahead so I cannot see his face. "Here's a scenic spot. Do you want to come down?" Xu asks.

"Sure."

He points at the pavilion ahead, shielded by an enormous gnarled sycamore tree. "That is called *money makes a ghost turn a millstone*." He buys some tokens and asks me, "Do you want to check it out?"

"Okay."

He pours half a dozen tokens into my palms. I drop them into the ghost's pouch. The hideous ghost starts turning the millstone and cackling, its wires snapping with electric sparks. Jin laughs loudly, as if it were funny.

"Sorry I missed your call," I whisper to Xu.

"No worries." He heads back to the car. "We have to hurry, if we want to beat the crowd going uphill."

We rush from one scenic spot to the next, as if it weren't a live mountain but an art museum. Xu waves off stalking guides, who beg to tell their stories about every rock, every stream. From a distance, I catch scraps of narration.

"This is the Thumb Rock. Does it look like your big thumb? That gentleman is right, it's a two-piece. You know why? Eh, Thunder God struck it in two. The thumb was naughty, so Thunder God *killed the chicken to frighten the monkey*, you know, punished it to warn others. . . ."

The story makes no sense. The rock, about forty feet high, towers aloft on a green mound—how is the giant like a thumb? I have long fingers that don't close up tightly. Mom said it was a sign I'd leave home to live in a faraway country, as she had left Wenzhou to study at a tech school with a scholarship. If Mom hadn't made her way out decades ago, I might've been born here into a peasant family.

"Actually I have relatives from this town," I tell Xu when we're back in the car. "My great-grandparents on my mother's side lived here. Mom brought me back once, when the last of my great-grandmothers passed away."

"Interesting," he says placidly. "I haven't told you before. My grandfather had an American wife, so I'm a quarter white. I was adopted—I don't know the details. As far as I'm concerned, my foster parents are my real parents, and Wenzhou is my hometown."

My mother once left Wenzhou in order to give us children a better life, whereas Xu is almost a naturalized foreigner in this town. Now I can see his chiseled features are not those of a typical southerner; his pale skin and dark hair are untouched by the southern sun. Was I attracted to his quarter of American, or to his three-quarters of Wenzhou, or to his well-mixed blood?

The summit is a broad plateau enclosed by a chained railing.

The majestic Guanyin shrine overlooks the valley—this must be the highest feng shui of the mountain. Jin takes a photo of Xu and me in front of the shrine. Xu buys a bundle of joss sticks and asks me if I want to honor Guanyin, the goddess of mercy and compassion.

"Not really," I reply.

A few pregnant women kneel, kowtow, and chant in front of the statue of Guanyin, praying for a son. They look silly.

"Come on, Rou, you're the guest from afar, your wishes may be granted."

He hands me a few joss sticks. I light them from the burning ones, stick them in the urn, press my palms together, and bow hastily so that I don't have time to think at all. The smoke makes me sneeze.

He repeats what I did with the remaining joss sticks, but slowly. His lips move soundlessly when he bows. I wish he weren't so secretive.

When his eyes open, I ask, "So what did you pray for?"

"Blessings." He's silent for a long while as if to gather himself. "I'm determined to make it in international business. It's the future of China."

"What about poetry?"

"I need to make money first; then, with some security, I may be able to sit down and write." He stares away from my right ear at the valley.

The terraced fields in the valley are winding like a maze. If I had brought my binoculars (which Sammy takes to see the ball games), I could ask Xu to point out where his home is. Following him back to the car, I notice that the bulges of his love handles beneath his black silk shirt spill over both sides of his brown leather belt. He looks complacent, like a married man. How come he doesn't mention his wife, as if she didn't exist?

On our way downhill, I press my forehead lightly on the back of his seat. "How's your wife?"

"She's at home."

"I wouldn't mind meeting her, if we have time."

"She never restricts my freedom," he replies. "I spend weeks at a time traveling for business. Work is my top priority. I seldom eat at home."

I cringe at his confession. Mom once said that wives were treated like breeders in Wenzhou. Since polygamy has become illegal, rich men nowadays keep mistresses. I shiver at the idea of becoming a mistress of a man who holds his wife in contempt.

Xu lowers the radio and talks to Jin in dialect. "We're going to have supper at the Crossroad Café," Xu tells me.

The tavern is located at an intersection, meaning that its owner is either poor or anti-superstition. Xu pours us some wine and begins to turn his cup around and around. The wind rises as the sky grows dim. Tractors drive by and raise more dust. A woman carrying a child comes to our table begging for some change. Xu looks away.

I suppress my disappointment and ask him, "Do you have kids yet?"

"A son." He looks at the baby inside the beggar's sling. "He's about this big."

"Congratulations!" I say. "It's better to have a son in Wenzhou, now with the one-child policy and all."

He grins with pride, still avoiding my eyes. "Yes, I get what I want."

It seems the right time for me to show him what I've gotten in the last few years. I take out my wallet, thumb through the cards, and pull out Sammy's picture.

"My boyfriend asked me to move in with him."

He glances at the photo and turns crimson from his face down to his neck. He tosses his head back to drain the wine in a loud gulp. Then his face becomes so pasty that blue veins stand out on his forehead.

"Congratulations," he says. All the warmth on his face is gone.

I lower my head and grip my wrist hard, until tears well up in my eyes. I want to feel some pain—pain is better than relief. Just when I know he did care for me, I lost him within an arm's reach.

"Why did you call me last night?" I ask him, letting my desperation come out like an accusation.

"What?"

"What did you call me about, you know, at the hotel?" I try to blink away my tears, feeling Jin's eyes sharp on me.

"I called to tell you to be ready at eight, and you were." His pale complexion has recovered; his eyes are tired and cold.

Xu and Jin talk in dialect and glance at me once a while. In the end, Xu tells me, "I have a client meeting tomorrow. Jin will take you to the airport."

Jin smiles at me, and I nod shyly.

We remain silent until we arrive at my hotel. "You need to check out in the morning. They take Visa. It's been a pleasure. Goodbye," he says, takes my hand, and drops it.

He walks away without looking back and disappears outside the revolving door. I stand in the lobby before the rockery fountain counting my blessings, that neither Xu nor I could drive, that his call didn't go through, and finally that he took offense at my love for Sammy even though he is married. I could've gone on loving him, had I not come closer to him and then broken up with him for good.

Sammy takes me back to his apartment, our home. We cook a big Chinese dinner with some mysterious ingredients that Mom gave me. We eat, then make love until the bed sheets are damp with our sweat. I feel like pouring out the passion that I had bottled up for Xu over the past five years. My wisdom came late, thanks to Xu, who was convinced of my love for Sammy even before I was.

"I missed you so much." I stamp his face with kisses. "Did you miss me?"

"No," he says. "I have Red Sox season tickets and never worried if I had to sleep in the sofa bed."

I giggle and pull his arm around my back. "I'm not moving out, and I'll renew my contract with Fidelity. If you throw me out, I'll camp in the living room, where you have to open the sofa bed for me."

He strokes my hair. "Have I ever thrown you out?"

"Not yet." I sigh. "I want to show you something." I get up and call him, "Come on, give me a hand."

"What?" he grumbles.

We pull the file cabinet out of the closet, and I unlock it. "I never throw away an old love letter. Here is all I have kept. You can look at them if you want."

He stares at me in disbelief, reaches into the cabinet, and pulls out the copy of my last Christmas card to Xu. He reads aloud, "*Right Here Waiting* is the theme song of my devotion, Dec. 1991." He throws the paper at me. "You hussy, explain this to me."

"He was my one and only ex. I had saved myself for him before I met you." I begin to tell him the whole story about Xu, how we met, how I had a crush on him for years, then how I went back to see him and showed off Sammy's picture to make him mad. "He was jealous because I love you. Are you asleep?" I shake him.

"What if he'd asked you to run away with him—what then?"

"To where?" He doesn't answer, as I stroke his closed eyelids. "We have no place to go. Don't you see? I came home."

"Should I open the sofa bed for you, hussy?" He presses me to his chest.

"I was jealous that you had an ex," I whisper into his ears. "Now I've got one, too, in China."

"Hussy and old Sammy broke up." He brushes my hair back with his fingers. "Honey, I'm your new boyfriend. Say goodbye to our exes." He kisses my face, turns off the light, and pulls the sheets over our warm bodies. We'll have to do laundry tomorrow.

A month later Xu sends me the photo of the two of us with a short note: "I was busy as hell when you visited last time. Now I have my driver's license. I wish I had driven you when you were down here. But there will be ample time. Please excuse my inattentiveness and feel welcome to revisit China."

I show the picture to Sammy and tease him, "He was your rival." Sammy calls me fickle. I say I'm safe now, dreamless.

He asks, "Am I not your dream?"

I kiss him, saying, "No, Sammy, you are my first love."

妹—What the Younger Daughter Falls For . . .

THE GOURMET

The sun has set, leaving its roseate footprints in the western sky. The tenants of the apartment building arrange their bamboo chairs alongside the asphalt sidewalk, enjoying the evening breeze. Middle-aged men, stripped to their waists, slap their palm fans against their hairy legs, chatting loudly about their raises, flat allotments, and pensions over a cacophony of screeching cicadas. Teenagers sit on wooden stools with their long legs bent back, arguing about which pop star will top China's billboard chart next week. I haven't heard of the names they call out.

My neighbor and her date sit knee to knee, with their backs to the crowd. She glows in her white embroidered blouse and yellow pleated skirt that hangs down to her ankles. The yellow ribbon in her hair flaps like a butterfly's wings. Once in a while, her bare-chested dad sits up from the bamboo chair to dart a watchful glance at the young couple.

I take a stroll with my dad while our dinner is being cooled at home under the ceiling fan. Mom is busy with some last-minute cleaning before my friend Amol arrives tonight. There was no stopping her from making a fuss, after she learned he is my colleague from Siemens Data Communications. I'll tour southern China with him during the next two weeks to wrap up my vacation.

Dad grabs my elbow and yanks me sideways to let a bicycle pass. Last week, when this first happened, I blamed my inattention on jet lag, but, in fact, I've grown to be a menace in Nanjing's traffic. After driving a car in the U.S. for three years, I've forgotten why I should make way for bicycles.

After a pause Dad says, "Is he a . . . *very* good friend of yours?"

"Very" isn't the right word. Amol is my only college friend, who also moved to Raleigh Research Triangle Park. For a while we dined out every Saturday and tried all the local restaurants. Most people on my team are now married, like Alice is. When she first joined my group, I went boot-shopping with her on Sunday. Then she found herself a boyfriend and started going to church. I took comfort in always having Amol to go hiking with when I wasn't in the mood to watch TV.

"Amol wants to tour China with me, that's all."

"Girl." Dad coughs up phlegm. I wince to hear him spit on the weeds by the sidewalk. "You're twenty-three years old. You know that's not all."

What else is there: attraction, sex? I had a couple of boy-friends in college, whom I haven't heard from since commencement. Not that I want to. I try not to miss the kind of easy love that is made in bed. After programming computers for a year, I've learned to be efficient, and the next thing I know, I've grown so sensitive to geographic distance that I'm even too lazy to chat with Alice, whose office is the third down the aisle from mine. Amol is an exception, though.

"Mom had my older sister when she was younger than I." Surprisingly, tears well up in my eyes. "I'm an old maid."

"What nonsense!" Dad points his palm fan at the crowd. My neighbor peers at us with a smile, while her date waves at us with his free hand. I wish Dad could act a little more discreetly while I'm a guest back in my hometown. "See these people? Do you think they turn their heads to admire my sallow cheeks?"

"Maybe they think I'm your date." I titter at his horrified eyes. It's the first joke I have made the whole week.

"Don't tell Mom that," he whispers in my ear.

I take his arm and lean my head on his shoulder. "Dad, I feel too old to be a girl but too young to be a woman. It's not fun."

He doesn't answer but squeezes my arm. "Tell me your friend's name again."

"Amol Bhattacharya."

"I hope he is a nice boy." He caresses the back of my hand, which snugs inside the crook of his arm.

The crowded dishes on the table make me feel full. The ceiling fan spins above our heads, humming like a giant insect. I dip my chopsticks into the greasy food, then wipe them on the edge of the bowl, biding my time. Amol's flight will arrive soon.

I tell Mom, "I really can't eat any more," and set down my chopsticks.

"What happened to your appetite?" Mom reaches out a hand to touch my forehead.

I lean back to leave her hand hanging in midair. "It's early morning back where I live, Mom." Then I wonder if this excuse has expired.

"Shouldn't you be having breakfast then?"

I take a sip of sour plum juice, the only thing I haven't grown tired of. "I don't have breakfast."

"You're not on a diet, I hope? Looking like a bean pole is not pretty, Lian, it's sickly."

Dad coughs loudly, no doubt to warn her, because they're a team, which is fine with me as long as they spare my feelings.

Mom goes on. "I like my baby to look plump. Plump is healthy, healthy is pretty."

I burst out laughing in a shrill voice that doesn't sound like mine. "So I'm not pretty. Well, who cares? I work with a computer. Why should I doll up? That won't get me a raise, won't get me anywhere, maybe a slap on my butt, which I definitely don't want."

Mom gapes at me. "I didn't say you aren't pretty. That's not what I meant."

I leave the table saying, "Fine," and dash into the bathroom to slam the door behind me. Be brave, I tell myself. I know better than to cry over spilt milk: for three years I've been homesick—now I feel lonelier than ever.

The door creaks open. I turn away to look at the yellow chrysanthemum prints on the shower curtain, tracing their golden petals that coil out like skinny fingers. Dad stands three feet behind me, filling the tiny room with his sober voice.

"You didn't need to throw a fit."

I try not to make a sound, breathing deeply.

"Your mom only wants the best for you. You can at least be appreciative of her effort."

I press my palms on my eyelids until I begin to see blue, red, and white blotches.

"Lian, your friend is here!" Mom shouts from the dining room.

Dad steps toward me when I reach out to take hold of the shower curtain, to clutch the slippery plastic. I hear him stop. Then the door thuds closed, and he's gone. I wash my face, rinse my mouth, and wipe myself dry on the towel. My eyes are pink and bleary as if I haven't slept for these two weeks.

Amol looks like a dark giant planted in the middle of our dining room, towering above my mother. His head is only inches under the ceiling fan, and his slouching shoulders seem foolish and out of place but are dear to my sight.

"Amol?" I call him.

He spins around, causing the bulk of his body to momentarily lose its balance.

"You're here!" I shout. With a laugh I wrap my arms around his stout back. He smells of a lightly pungent perfume.

"How are you, Lian?" He brushes my elbows with his fingertips.

I squeeze him hard, then let him go. If Mom had not been watching us, I would've realized the day is really too hot for hugging.

"Has he eaten?" Mom asks in a timid voice. I translate.

Amol rubs his palms. "They gave me some extra salty peanuts on the plane. I have to wash my hands first."

I take him to the bathroom and give him a new towel. Mom has cleaned the table when I return.

"Are you done?" I ask her, surprised.

"Yes, we were waiting for you."

I march to the kitchen to pick out two tofu dishes and chives with scrambled eggs, and fill a bowl with rice. We have no silverware in the house, and Amol cannot use chopsticks, so I grab a porcelain spoon and plate.

"Why don't you take out some meat dishes?" Mom asks. "Your friend will think we're stingy."

"He doesn't eat meat," I tell her.

"Then how did he grow so tall?"

I ignore her.

"It's a miracle for a flight to be an hour and half ahead of schedule." Amol's loud voice echoes in the bathroom. "Fortunately I had a first-class ticket, or my bones would've been hurting after crouching in the seat for twenty hours." He stomps out with his sleeves rolled up to his elbows, showing his hairy forearms. "It's so good to see you again," he says with water on his grinning face. "I missed you at work."

"What did he say?" Mom asks.

I pull out a chair to invite Amol to sit down. "Mom, I can't carry on a conversation if you ask me to translate everything."

Amol thanks me. "Has your mom said something about me?" he whispers to me.

"Yes." I smile. "She wishes you a good appetite. That will make her happy."

Dad carries out two bamboo chairs and nudges Mom toward the door. "Wife, let's go out to enjoy the breeze. Leave the kids to have their talk."

I watch Mom close the screen door very slowly and latch the iron burglarproof gate with a click. I wait for her face to pop back and have a last peek. Instead, their footsteps recede. I turn to Amol and smile with relief. He has mixed the dishes with rice on the plate, picking up the food with his nimble fingers.

He shows me the spoon. "It's a little thick on the bottom, hard for me to handle the chives."

"It's a soup spoon." I put it aside.

It is late. Outside, the mosquito-repellent incense has gone out. The scent of sweet olive and yulan magnolia drifts into the bedroom. Sitting on the windowsill, I watch people drag their chairs into the building, making hollow echoes in the stairway. Our iron gate is unlocked, then clicks closed. My parents have returned.

"Lian?" Mom calls from the hallway. "Why didn't you turn on the lights?"

"Hush," I say. "Amol is sleeping in his room."

"Good!" she exclaims, then covers her mouth with her palm fan. "I mean, it's good that you treat a guest with courtesy," she says in a strained low voice.

I put my feet on the cover of the sewing machine, feeling the fuzzy flannel under my soles. Mom puts the bamboo chair in the living room, then switches on the ceiling light. The fluorescent light stings my eyes.

"Your dad and I agree the west room is too hot for you to sleep in tonight. He lends us ladies this south room, and he'll take your oven room."

"Mom, I'm okay."

"See for yourself." She backs into the hallway. "Then tell us where you'd rather sleep tonight."

I put on slippers and follow her to the west room. Mom is right. Sitting on the warm bamboo mat, I feel sweat seep through my pores.

"Thanks, Dad," I murmur.

He hands me my pillow and pink throw and plops his brown towel on the mat. "See you ladies in the morning. And no quarreling."

Mom taps his arm as we head out.

I kneel on my parents' wedding bed to fan the corners of the mosquito net, making the white gauze puff out and suck in with each wave. Mom tucks in the net under the bamboo mat, and clamps the netting door with three wooden clips, on the top, middle, and bottom.

Mom pulls my pillow to align with hers against the head-board. I lie down, aware of the half-foot gap between us. She swings her legs aside, making the bamboo mat bend under me. The gauze net quivers above us in a breeze.

"Your friend looks awfully tanned," Mom says. "Has he got-ten a lot of sun?"

"Amol is Indian, you know."

"He has long hairs on his arms, and he eats with his hands."

I shake my head angrily, making the pillow crunch under my neck.

"Other than that, he's not bad-looking. But I'm worried he's such a big man, and you're a fine-boned skinny girl. The marital life. . . ."

Mom stops short because I burst out laughing. For three years I haven't heard "the marital life" as a euphemism for sex. I press my face on the pillow and let the fine bamboo mat squeeze a few tears out of my eyelids.

"What's tickling your funny bone?" Mom rubs my shoulder blade. "You see what I'm getting at."

I pick my head up from the pillow. "What *do* you mean, Mom? That he's too much a man for me?"

"He's a big fellow."

"Well, I've had *boyfriends!*"

The air seems to freeze inside the mosquito net for a minute. Then I smell the delicate aroma of sweet olive and yulan magnolia. The scent raises gooseflesh on my arms.

"You've never told me." Mom pounds the mat with her cupped hand. "I feel like an old fogy!"

I blush to the roots of my hair. "I have *never,* with Amol."

"How were *they?*" she asks, wide-eyed like a child.

I roll away from her as far as I can go, until the mosquito net covers my face like a gauze mask. I suck a patch of cloth between my teeth, tasting the clean gauze.

"They're only human, Mom. Only human."

By ten o'clock the morning heat is on the rise. Amol's door remains shut. Mom takes our dirty dishes to the sink. Dad slaps the rolled-up newspaper at a fly on the table but misses it.

"How's the weather?" I ask him.

"Weather? Oh, weather." He opens the paper and puts it at an arm's length to read, "Sunny, partly cloudy in the afternoon, high 38°C."

With a nod I smooth down the skirt over my shins. "Dad, Amol wants to go to the farmers' market with us today."

"Oh, yes," Mom echoes from the kitchen. "He would like to help us with lunch." She grins at us.

"If he doesn't sleep until sunset," Dad mutters under his breath.

The door of Amol's room thuds open to bump against the wall. Amol stands wearing only his striped pajama pants. "Good morning," he says, dazed and perplexed. With his large hairy chest, he reminds me of an enormously cuddly teddy bear.

I leap off the bench to open the bathroom door for him. "It's all yours, Amol. Take your time." He thanks me and then closes the door.

I poke my head into his room. The white throw is piled in the middle of the bed, which is obviously too small for him. Dad nudges me on the shoulder. "You go get dressed, Lian. Let me take care of this bit of housework."

I pinch both sides of my skirt to fan it out like a peacock's tail. "But I'm dressed, Dad, for going to the market anyway. We won't drop into an opera house on the way, will we?"

"Don't be naughty with your dad." Mom presses her lips together to conceal a smile.

Dad shifts his gaze from my face to Mom's, then back to mine, as if trying to uncover some mystery. Maybe Mom hasn't told him about my "premarital life," although I cannot imagine her keeping a secret like that. He backs up a step to take my whole figure into his view, then steps forward to pull out my jade pendant by its necklace.

"It ought to be worn like this. See how green the jade has become. It's pretty."

I bend my head to my chest and am appalled by what I see. "Dad, pink clashes with green, making me look like a country girl." I slide the jade behind the dress.

"Too much skin is shown here." He gestures at my chest. "It's up to you."

Dad folds Amol's white throw to put under the pillow. He wipes the empty ashtray with his finger. Amol doesn't smoke.

Dad picks up the computer book at the foot of the bed to lay it on the open suitcase. The cleaning is done.

Amol sings in the shower, wobbly and indistinct at first, then forming the phrase "Thank you, frailty." Amidst the splashing water, he bellows out a stream of "Thank you, thank you, thank you," obviously losing track of his lyrics.

The farmers' market, under the teal plastic awning, is packed with fresh produce, a feast for my eyes. Flies bounce from pile to pile. A mosquito brushes by my ear, buzzing like a mini helicopter. I try not to touch the sweating skins around me, keeping my eyes on Amol, who moves swiftly in the crowd.

"Wait for me," I call to him.

"I want to tell you a secret." Amol strides ahead to leave my parents behind and out of earshot. "I felt drowsy after dinner last night, and thought it was the jet lag. This morning I was having breakfast and tasted MSG in the bean curd. I'm allergic, you know."

"No wonder!" I say. "I was always thirsty and drank tons of juice, then I didn't want to eat anything. Mom thought I was on a liquid diet."

"Diet? She has no idea what a good eater you are."

I sniff the sweet scent of fish blood and pinch my nose.

Amol stops at a counter where a dozen carps float on the shallow water in a wooden basin. He flips open a gill cover. "Bloody red, it's practically alive," he says and picks up the carp from the murky water. "This will make a kick-ass maacher jhol." Meeting my eyes, he explains, "It's a Bengali dish. Wait and see; it will make you eat."

The peasant girl hooks the carp on her steelyard.

"Wait, take your pinkie off that scale!" Mom yells behind me. "You're so young, who taught you to be dishonest?"

The girl nudges the sliding weight with her finger and thumb, her cheeks burning so red they seem to blend in with her kerchief.

Mom carries on. "Don't you take us for big-nosed foreigners! Let me tell you, this is our daughter, and here is her friend—"

"Mom, have you said enough?" I wrap my arm around her shoulders and shake her a little. "It's just a carp."

Amol watches us curiously.

I explain to him, "She's trying to get us a good deal."

"I see, bargaining. Is she successful?"

"Very."

Mom squats down to watch the girl clean the carp, making sure she doesn't cut off too much meat along with the fins. The floor before her shoe-tips is spotted with fish scales and blood, but Mom doesn't flinch. The girl presses the carp into a basin of bloody water to rinse it off. Still hunkering down, Mom offers her basket as if accepting a prize. Then she clutches my arm to stand up. Her fingers pinch my flesh for an instant, and I realize how old Mom has grown during the years we've been apart.

I grab Amol's wrist before he drifts off again. "Let's just get the ingredients," I tell him. "It's almost one o'clock, and they must be hungry."

"Of course." Amol puts a hand on my back as if escorting me. "I'll make it quick."

I feel a smile bend the corners of my lips.

I feed Mom a taste of tomato chutney and watch her face screw into a frown. "This is the sauce," I tell her with a giggle. Then I wrap up the bowl and put it into the fridge to chill.

"I ought to cook it with mustard oil," Amol says. "But here I'll have to be creative." He pours half a soup spoon of peanut oil into the skillet and turns on the gas stove, then adds a pinch of mustard seeds. "I'm making my own mustard oil, with a dab of peanut aroma. This is getting fun."

I coat the fish head in turmeric and salt mix. The mustard seeds begin to pop in the lidded skillet. "Do you want me to chop a piece of ginger?" I ask. "It helps reduce the fishy smell."

He sends the coated fish pieces into the hot oil, where the fish skin sizzles with the delicious smell of the spices and flesh. "There's always a better way to do something," he says. "Turmeric does the trick with the odor. Not only that, it also provides a yellow color and will bind the fish properly during the frying."

The carp turns opaque and juice seeps out. He turns the fish pieces over, and the sizzling grows louder. "Turmeric is a spice of many uses," he says. "Indian women use its paste as an exfoliator, you know, to polish their skin."

"Wow." I hesitate for a few seconds. "How come you never asked me to cook with you on the weekend? You could've taught me a few recipes so I could show off to my parents."

"I didn't think you'd be interested."

"Did I ever tell you that?"

"No." He removes the cooked fish pieces and puts in the last batch along with the fish head. "You always looked so fresh and neat, as if you had just stepped out of a beauty salon. I didn't want you to dirty your shirt and smell like a kitchen."

"Me? I only wear jeans and sneakers!"

"Yes, but your sneakers are bleached and you iron your jeans. You put together casual outfits with great care so you can look like a team player." He smiles at me. "I can tell you don't really want to dress like one of the guys."

I flush to the roots of my hair. The kitchen temp must be nearing a hundred degrees.

"I have to confess," he begins. I can hear the thumping of my own heart as I wait for his next word. "I miss eating carp heads. It's the best part of a carp, you know, which I always claim at home, but I've never seen it served at any restaurant."

I censor an awkward smile. What else was I expecting? I chide my own silliness. We're cooking a carp and having a good time, which ought to satisfy me.

"Can I have the tail?" I ask. "I'm the baby in the family, the tail eater."

"Of course." He adds more peanut oil and mustard seeds to the skillet. "Bengalis who can't afford a whole carp often buy the tail and head of a carp and flavor dishes with them, just to get the taste of fish."

"Chinese do that, too, and we have an auspicious name—having a beginning and an end." I lean against the kitchen counter. "We're not that different, are we?"

"Certainly not. We're both Asians, educated in Florida, working for a German company, living in North Carolina, and vacationing in China." He adds the black mustard paste and salt, two green chilies, and a bowl of water. "When it boils," he tells me, "lower the heat to simmer. I'll be right back."

I watch him disappear into the bathroom. "Mom, isn't he something?"

Mom tastes a piece of lily flower in her scallop casserole, then pops open a can. "Needs a dab of gourmet powder," she murmurs.

I snatch away the can. "It's called MSG, Mom, a harmful chemical banned in many restaurants. You shouldn't keep this in the house." I gesture to toss it into the trash.

"Why, I've been using it all my life!"

"Not on my carp, no way!"

When the high-pressured cooker gives off a loud whistle, I drop the can on the counter. Our dessert soup is ready.

"I thought I heard a train." Amol makes his way back to the stove. "We're almost done."

"Been cooking for half an hour, and giving me orders," Mom mutters to herself. "Don't you chemical me. Wait and see who's the gourmet."

The maacher jhol, as Amol calls it, is a pale yellow dish with a slightly pungent taste imparted by the ground mustard. Watching Amol savor the head, I wish I had asked him to share half of it. Next time, I'll be bolder. I scrape the tail with the rest of the sauce, eating it with the same indulgence as he does the head, licking each finger after picking out a bone. Having cleaned the plate, I pour a spoonful of tomato and onion chutney onto my rice and wolf it down.

"Good girl, you're finally eating." Mom laughs loudly.

"I should've cooked two carps," Amol says regretfully. I translate.

"It's the best to be 80 percent full, and still wanting," Dad says. "It makes the next meal even more desirable."

I tell that to Amol, and he chuckles. "Tell your parents I look forward to cooking for them again, because they paid me an honest compliment."

"He laughs just like one of us." Mom watches Amol eat and smacks her own lips.

Afternoon sunlight slants across the kitchen counter. Outside, a fly keeps bumping against the window screen. Dad leans over to turn up the ceiling fan.

"Is everyone ready for dessert?" he asks.

"Wait for me," I say.

"Why 80 percent full?" Mom scolds. "Let Lian eat to her capacity! I want her to eat to 120 percent if she can."

Dad raises his hands in surrender.

I finish my last morsel. "It's not just that I'm slow," I tell my parents. "I've been talking a lot, like, for four mouths. That's not true: I only translated the nice things you guys said, but I listened with eight ears. Well, not really, because you hear everything, too. So, I talked with three mouths and listened with two ears, ate with one mouth and two hands." I lick my fingers again, then wipe them on the napkin.

Dad pats me on the back. "You don't have to explain, Lian; we know you from head to toe." He gets up to serve us the iced dessert.

I look into my lap wondering what he was alluding to.

"Is it true he didn't use the gourmet powder?" Dad asks.

"Yes," I reply. "The taste is in the spices: mustard seeds, turmeric, and chilies. We were missing a few items like bay leaf, cilantro, and mustard oil, but he improvised. I love the sauces in Indian dishes—they're rich but not filling."

"It's never too late to learn a new recipe," Dad says with his back to us.

Mom darts me a gleeful glance and gets up to pass us the dessert bowls.

Amol tastes his dessert soup. "This is too good!" he exclaims. "I haven't had lotus seeds for ages."

Pride lights up Mom's face when she hears me. "Lian, tell

him this dessert soup is composed of lotus seeds, mung beans and tremella, sugar, and a touch of cornstarch. This summer tonic allays the internal heat in the body."

"Thank you, Mama." Amol presses his palms together. I don't need to translate this. With her face flushed with pleasure, Mom seems to have grown five years younger.

"A balanced meal contains all five flavors," Dad says, "sweet, sour, salty, bitter, and pungent, together creating harmony in the body."

"One, two, three, four, five harmonies." Amol scoops five lotus seeds into his mouth. "With a sip of tonic juice, ah, I'm balanced."

His elbow glides across the table corner, touching the back of my hand. I don't move and wait for his eyes to find mine. "We have twelve days of vacation," I tell him, "all to ourselves."

We lean back in our chairs at the same time. When I reach out to take hold of a table leg, his tanned fingers ascend the pole to touch my palm.

母—What the Mother Is Afraid Of . . .

MY OLD FAITHFUL

As soon as I set foot in the nursery's garden I find the auspicious flower: a red double peony. Its huge blossoms burst forth as if brimming over with rose-red joy. I stand in awe, while the store clerk tells me its strong stems never fall, even in the harshest weather. Its name, Old Faithful, makes it perfect for my home, as my husband and I are going to have our thirtieth wedding anniversary in two weeks.

"Yes," I say.

I carry the potted peony to the storefront. My husband is talking to a young woman with a fluffy, chrysanthemum-like hairdo. "Can you give me a hand?" I call out to him. The woman glances at me, backs away into the crowd, and boards the bus.

My husband takes my heavy pot and clamps it onto the back seat of his bike. "You scared away some business," he tells me with a smile.

"What sort of business?"

"The bawdy kind." He crisscrosses the pot with a nylon rope and fastens a dead knot. "I'm pretty sure she was a prostitute."

"You mean she wanted *you?*"

He pushes the bike onto the sidewalk. "Am I not a man? Don't I have a wallet?"

"Watch your mouth!"

I feel a sharp pain in my back and grab the seat of his bike. My fibroids are acting up again. I've had them for more than ten years; now I am beginning to have belly and back pains. My husband took me to the hospital this morning, and the doctor suggested I have a hysterectomy—to have both my uterus and ovaries removed. It's a safe procedure, she told me, and many women who have had it are very happy with the results. I told her I had to think about it. Upset, I left the hospital with the single thought that I'd buy something nice to cheer me up. I found the Old Faithful, but what's the use of that if my husband is bent on ruining my day?

"You carry on like this, and make sure that bad luck follows my heels," I accuse him.

"Take it easy." He holds my hand and squeezes it gently. "She wants business and we don't, so there's no transaction, end of story."

I watch the crowd move in the street. Young men and women dress in white, fawn, lavender, and dark summer outfits that bring out their radiant faces. No one knows I am about to lose my uterus, with which I have carried three children. My older daughter is expecting a baby, and my younger daughter is getting married to an Indian man. My son is dating a professional dancer, who seems to think herself too pretty for him. Not that I care much for young people's folly, but here I stand on the sidewalk in the midday sun, feeling stranded on an island of youth with my old man.

"Look at you!" I stroke his sunken cheek, his lusterless skin. "You're not too wrinkled for a fifty-three-year-old, I guess."

He wraps his arm around my waist, and pushes the bike with his free hand. "Wife, you're a shapely fifty-one-year-old."

As far as I can remember, I placed only one bet in my whole life—to choose a man and marry. Based on the Gregorian calendar, my husband's birthday was in early July and mine was in late July. However, according to the lunar calendar, we were born on the same day and hour but two years apart, which I took as a good omen when we started out. Back then he couldn't afford to take me to a good eating house. There was a peony tree near where he lived, so he brought me a white peony on our first date. I kept it in a pink enamel cup for over a month until it withered. Its petals became brittle and eventually broke to pieces. We were married a year later on our lunar birthday. The sweet scent of peony permeated our new home. Ten months later we had our first daughter. From then on we celebrated our anniversary in place of our lunar birthday. We were blessed with a son and a younger daughter in years to come. Bringing up three children nearly took all that we had; I never owned a tube of lipstick until my children left home. Yet every year I bought a half-dozen cut peonies to celebrate our anniversary. Today, for the first time in thirty years, I allowed myself to buy a specimen plant.

I unlock the apartment door and let my husband carry the potted peony inside. "Was she good-looking?" I ask casually.

"Who?"

I drop my keys, which fall noisily onto the dining room table. "The woman you met at the bus stop, in front of the floral shop."

"I've forgotten her face."

"Times have really changed." I kick off my pumps and slide into my cloth slippers. "There wasn't a divorced family in our neighborhood until ten years ago. Now a hooker can approach my husband in broad daylight, when I turn my head for ten minutes." I sit on the sofa and watch him take the watering can from our balcony.

"I have to tell you a story." He brushes my knee with his fingers as he passes me on his way to the kitchen. "Once upon a time, an old monk and his disciple went to cross a puddle, where they found a beautiful woman who was stranded. The young disciple chanted, 'Amitābha, may Buddha preserve us,' so that he wouldn't be tempted." My husband raises his voice as water pours into the can. "The old monk went ahead without a word and carried the woman over the puddle. The disciple was distressed by his master's action, but didn't dare to voice his opinion. Then, after a long while, the disciple couldn't stand the silence anymore and asked, 'How could you, my master, carry a woman in your arms?' Surprised, the old monk replied, 'I put her down long ago. Are you still carrying her?'"

I don't smile but peer at myself in the armoire mirror. People always said how young I looked, until last year, when I stopped having my periods. I haven't gotten more wrinkles, but my skin has lost its sheen and become a little rubbery. Every morning after I wash, I have to rub in a palmload of cream to keep my skin from feeling tight on my face. I pat my cheeks and suck them in to make myself a pointed chin.

My husband turns off the faucet and carries the watering can into the living room. "What I don't get is how a wise woman like you, who has raised three grown children and is a worshiper of Guanyin, can get jealous over a prostitute?"

"Jealous? Get over yourself!" I get up to take the watering can from his hands. "I was worried about you, who might be tempted." I'm about to say "by a young chick," but I don't feel like reminding him about the hooker, so I try a figurative expression: "by the weeds at the roadside." I mist the peony, its bright red blossoms and dark green leaves. If only my skin could plump up with water and glisten like that.

"Is this a good plant?"

"The best: it's called Old Faithful." I put the watering can on the floor and stand up to push my fist into the small of my back. "The kind of peony that creates good feng shui for a married life by counteracting bad influences from the streets."

He lies on the sofa and leers at me. "Teach me more."

I stride over to hit his hand. "Be serious! She's an expensive specimen."

"Are you sure it's a she?"

"She blooms like a lady." I sit on the sofa and lean my head against his shins. "When the dew seeps into the bud, the peony flower opens like a bride to her groom."

He jolts my head lightly with his knees. "Dirty talk."

His shins open and I drop onto his stomach. I say with a laugh, "Aren't you a little concerned I'm going to lose the potent organs in my belly?" I slide a hand to lace my fingers with his.

He pulls me up to lie on his chest. "Yes." I stiffen a little, waiting for him to continue. "Our children ought to be here and help me look after their mother." He reaches his hand down to my belly and rubs it with his palm. "But I'll do my best to be your nursemaid, and make sure that you recover through and through."

I let out a long breath that I didn't know I was holding. Then I lay my hand on top of his to rub my belly with him in slow circles. I can feel the dry warmth of his palm.

When Saturday comes, I help my husband sort the new survey forms for his youth unemployment study. For the first time in months, he gives me a handful of forms with one-inch Polaroid headshots instead of the booklets of psychological test results. It's nice for me to match a face with a form. I thumb through the stack of paper with interest. Suddenly one photo makes my eyes pop. I fold its corner and peer at my husband, who carries the watering can and a basket into the yard.

"Skip the peony," I tell him. "It needs to stay dry."

I study the form, certain that I've found a culprit, then bring the sheet to him in the yard. "Do you recognize her?"

He unfolds the corner of the paper with his wet fingers. "Who is she?"

I wave the form in his face. "Do you really not know her?"

"I designed the study, and my grad students helped me with the research. I've never met her."

"Oh, yes, you did." I prod his temple. "She asked you to do a certain business with her."

He snatches the form to have a closer look. "Her hair was different, wasn't it?"

She looks bald with her hair pulled back tightly in a ponytail. There's nothing sultry about her, except for the maroon lipstick on her mouth.

"She ought to be disqualified," I say.

"Why?"

"Well, doesn't she have a job already, a business, as you call it?"

"She's one of the twenty-five finalists in my survey pool, which started out six months ago with more than a thousand subjects." He hands the form back to me. "We want to recommend her to the employment agency."

"But a prostitute belongs in jail."

"It so happens she also belongs to an expensive study." My husband snaps off the daylily blooms, which he'll use to make an appetizing soup for me. "There're so many young women from the countryside who don't hold salaried jobs in Nanjing that it's hard for us to track them down and get the statistics. I need her for a final interview before sending her away."

I want to tell him she's trouble, but I'm afraid he'll laugh at me for being jealous. What have I got to be jealous of? Nothing at all. I've only slept with one man in my life, and I'm almost an old woman. But the photo doesn't show me an attractive woman. With a pug nose and a thin yellow face, the prostitute looks underfed and sleepy, and nowhere near as pretty as my pregnant daughter who was born the same year as she was. Last night I browsed through my daughter's photos on her website. Getting heavier each week, she looks like a pampered child with her soft plump cheeks. But this woman, Sui, if that's her real name, wanted to sleep with my husband for money. In other words, she intended to rob our family bank by opening her legs.

I take the form and roll it up. "If she means that much to your study, can I do you a favor and interview her for you?"

"You know we welcome free labor, so long as you put on your kind, motherly face and ask them our list of questions. Don't be creative." He puts the watering can on the ground. "Next Saturday, be on time."

I cover my mouth with my hand, because it'll be our birthday and anniversary. I'd give anything to avoid bad luck on that day, but I have no choice. I'd rather suffer it out myself than have the trollop go near my husband again. I stamp my foot so hard that I nearly crush a daylily.

"Fine."

"Not so fast." He grabs my hand. "You have to interview all my subjects because I don't want interviewer variation in my data."

"Maybe I'll start off by asking this woman how unemployed she really is."

My husband reaches up and pinches my bottom. I slap away his hand and run back inside. What if our neighbors see us? Sometimes he picks the wrong place to be funny.

By Saturday, my back pain is worse. I take a strap-on cushion with me to the interview office. After my first subject leaves, I walk out from behind my desk and try my husband's sofa chair, which has a cushioned back but is set at an awkward angle that forces me to sit straight. I give up and call in my second subject. The office is so spacious that I hear my voice echo in the room.

The interview is easy when all the subjects are eager to cooperate as potential job applicants. The pile of forms diminishes on my desk like a sycamore tree shedding leaves in the autumn wind. I'm reluctant to find that the prostitute's form appears at the bottom of the stack.

I cross my fingers and study her photo, while I hear my stomach grumble. I push her form aside and step outside to the snack counter to buy a scallion pancake. I should save my appetite for our anniversary dinner tonight, when my son is coming to see us. But I feel like avoiding the woman who pestered my husband. Back in the office, I chew every bite of my pancake as slowly as I can, and pick at the pieces of green onion.

I hear a knock on the door. "Yes?" I ask with a full mouth.

"I'm wondering if it's my turn," a soft voice says.

I sip tea to wash the food down. "Come on in."

The doorknob turns and the door opens. A small woman steps inside and finds me behind the desk. She pulls her red jacket around herself.

"I've waited for a long time."

"Right." I wipe my mouth with a napkin. "The interview only takes a few minutes."

She wears slacks and a jacket, so I can't tell if she has a good figure. A red kerchief covers her hair, except for a strand of curly bangs that hangs above her brows. Her hips appear amazingly pliant as she sits in the chair and crosses her legs. She peers up at me.

I look down to read the first question on the list, "Miss Sui, your personality test shows you may have the potential to become a shop assistant. What are your interests in sales?"

"I can do papercuts. I learned that when I was a little girl." As she smiles, I notice her almond-shaped eyes are rather pretty.

"Good." I mark my sheet. "How many years of papercutting experience have you had?"

"Longer than I had school." She wipes her thigh with the back of her hand as if dusting her slacks. "I finished elementary school, then started to work with my grandparents and supported my younger sister for school."

"Doing what?" Startled by my loud voice, I clear my throat.

"My granddad grew peonies and harvested their roots for medicine, but the money was never enough." I screw and unscrew the cap of my pen as she talks. "I made papercuts during New Years. Then they went out of fashion, because people can afford flannel drapes or stained glass nowadays. After my sister graduated from high school, I came to Nanjing to look for a city job." She pushes a finger under her kerchief to tuck in the loose bangs. "But no one would hire me because I don't have a city residence card."

My pen slips from my fingers and rolls to the edge of the desk before I grab it. "Where are your parents?" The question is not on my list.

"My dad died, and my mom remarried. One day she took us to our grandparents, and I never saw her again." She waves her hand in front of her face as if to drive away a fly. "She's dead, too, for all I care."

I chew the end of my pen, hesitant to sign the job candidate form. I don't know how many lies she has told me, but I'm not a judge of her life. I'm only a bank accountant. I was an abacus expert before the electronic calculator days, and have mentored young college graduates in my career. I don't know what it is like to live by one's wit and charm; I've always depended on my skills.

I rip a page from my notepad, find a pair of scissors, and pass them to her. "Do a papercut for me," I tell her.

She smoothes out the paper. "It's the wrong color."

"What?"

"I use red paper."

I check every drawer but cannot find any colored paper. "Just cut it."

She folds the paper once, and chops her scissors into it. "I did it all wrong," she says and opens the cut paper. "I should've turned the paper, not the scissors. Can I have another page?"

"Well, can't you fix the curve?"

"The fix-up always shows." She tears the paper. "It's better to do another."

I rip another sheet and hand it to her.

She folds the paper and studies it for a moment. Then she presses the scissor blades into the sheet to cut a long curve. She sighs. "No good. Can I have another?"

I give her my whole letter pad.

She cuts and tears, tears and cuts some more. Finally, she opens up a white pattern. I stoop a bit to look at it against her red coat. "What is it?"

"A longevity peach."

I press my chest against the desk to study the peach pattern, when a dull cramp rises in my belly as if baby feet were stomping inside my bowels. I lean back in my chair and squeeze my stomach with both hands.

Sui rises from her chair.

"It's nothing, just a chronic woman's thing," I tell her. "Come, show me the papercut."

Sui presses the paper on my desk. It's a plump peach with small leaves attached to a stem. "I haven't done papercuts in a long time," she says. "My hands are rusty."

"No." I sit up a little as the cramp eases. "You said you wanted a perfect cut, so you made one. This is good, honest work. You can make a living with such a skill."

She clasps her hands and smiles. "It doesn't make money."

Before I can think, I reach into my purse and pull out a ten-yuan bill. "I'd like to buy this." Her eyes are glued to the bill. "Or what do you think is a fair price?"

She bites her lip and cups her cheek in her hand. For a while, I feel more ashamed than she is, but I cannot take it back now. I hold up the bill higher. "It is fair, ma'am," she whispers. "But I cannot give you a white peach, it's bad luck." She takes the papercut and returns to her seat, and leaves my hand hanging in midair. "I'll paint it and mail it to you."

I put my hand down, but I don't want to give her my address. "I live at a place where mail gets lost all the time," I lie to her. "Maybe we should meet somewhere. How about tomorrow noon at the floral shop in front of the Number 7 bus station?"

She nods like a pecking chick. "If you still want it, you can pay me then."

"We're done for today. Thank you." I sign her job candidate form, then turn around to unstrap the cushion on my chair.

I'm scrubbing my hands with a luffa sponge when my son calls out from the table, "Mom, the spring rolls are getting cold!"

"You can start."

I dry my hands with a towel, rub on a little Pond's cream, then go to sit down at the table. My husband and son have moved the potted peony onto the dining table, where it takes up a whole side. The three of us huddle in a semicircle in front of the food and the flower.

"The weirdest thing happened to me today," I say and push the vinegar saucer to the middle. "I offered ten yuan to a woman who wanted to do a certain business with your dad."

My son dips a spring roll in vinegar, then bites into it. Its crispy skin falls off in pieces.

"Your mom is too much." My husband picks up the broken skin from the vinegar with his chopsticks, then dips his spring roll into it. "A prostitute talked to me two weeks ago, and she's still punishing me."

"I wasn't." I press his wrist. "I offered to buy her papercut of a longevity peach. She wouldn't let me have it because it was white."

My son has finished his first roll and reaches for a second. "Country folks used to cut white paper money for dead people," he says.

I slap his hand. "Watch your mouth! Have you forgotten what day it is?"

My son raises his wine cup. "Happy anniversary, Mom and Dad!" We drink up, and he refills his cup.

My husband rips the shell lid off a river snail, pokes a chopstick into its opening, then sucks its curly meat out in a loud slurp. He fixes his eyes on the snail bowl as he chews. "It's done just right, not raw, nor overdone."

"I bumped into a prostitute one night at a bus stop," my son says. "I told her the last bus was coming in twenty minutes. She said, 'Twenty minutes? Ten is enough!'"

In spite of myself, I burst into laughter with them.

"Mom, have you decided about the hysterectomy?"

I nod. "The doctor is right, I know. But I need a little time to think it over. I want to understand what's happening before I have my insides ripped out of me."

"Seventy to eighty percent of women have fibroids," my son says. "It's nothing to be nervous about."

I don't see any sense in talking about fibroids with my son, even though he is a dentist. "How're you getting on with your girlfriend?" I ask him.

"I caught her leering at our neighbor's husband." He licks away a drop of sauce from the corner of his mouth. "All she cares about is the latest fashion. I'm through with carrying shopping bags for her like a porter."

My husband folds the ruffled napkin inside out to wipe his mouth, so that he doesn't waste a new napkin. "Watch out, son. A frivolous woman can bring instability, even sorrow onto a household."

I say quietly, "But you don't know her reasons." Likewise, I haven't learned how Sui, the country girl, became the prostitute who tempted my husband.

"What reason?" My son puts his fist to his mouth and belches quietly. "I'm crazy about her, so she takes me for a joke. I've had it."

The odor of fried spring rolls mixes with the salty smell of river snails. I should've used an extra fan when I cooked. Now a light blue smoke stings my eyes. I walk over to pull open the curtains and let cool evening air pour inside.

"Are you into papercutting now, Mom?"

"She couldn't go back to fix anything because it would've shown, so she had to do it right in one cut, like peeling an apple. It was pretty amazing." I walk back to the table. "It made me think of family. No one can choose what family you want to be born into, but it sure makes a person out of you, doesn't it? A good beginning is half of the success, and vice versa."

My son shakes his head. "Snooty, Mom."

"I'd be grateful if I were you." I take hold of his chin in my hand. "Look at you, all grown up, stout, healthy, and well educated, a twenty-seven-year-old dentist, good-looking and clean-cut. Why do you worry about a dancer who doesn't love you?"

He breaks into a shy smile. "When you put it like that—"

"She's serious." My husband pulls my hand away from my son's face. "If you ask for her advice on dating, she'll tell you to give the woman a peony instead of going shopping with her."

"Why not?" I raise my voice. "Then you can tell right away if she's into you or your money. Peony is the flower of riches and honor, and it creates good feng shui towards finding a faithful and loving partner."

"Really, Dad?"

My husband nods very slowly, as if his head were too heavy for his neck to bear.

"Mom, should I buy a peony, too? I can use some good feng shui in my life."

I smile. "Let me check it out for you tomorrow."

"To Mom, Dad, and Old Faithful!" He raises his wine cup, clinks our cups in turn, then reaches out his arm to clink his wine cup with the peony pot.

I lift my cup and add, "To our daughters in the U.S.!"

"Health and prosperity to us all!" my husband toasts.

Then we toss our heads back to drink up. I feel my mind relax, as the alcohol oozes down my throat. This is life, I remind myself, to have our daughters prosper abroad, and our son live nearby so that he can drop in to have dinner with us when we miss him. Yet our family would be complete if my daughters were with us.

The next day on my way to the bus stop I buy a thin stack of red paper, and regret it as soon as I step outside the art supply store into the hot sun. What was I thinking to make an appointment with a prostitute? As if she would listen to me like my daughter. In all likelihood, I could bring a policeman with me. I only need to point my finger at her, and she'd be busted. In fact, she may've been snatched off the street and thrown into a prison already. I quicken my steps toward the bus stop.

The bus unloads and loads more people, then takes off. There's no sign of her. I hold up the red paper to shield my eyes from the midday sun as I read the bus sign. The next bus is due in a half hour.

I stroll into the floral shop, fanning myself with the red paper. In the garden I catch sight of Sui, who props her hands on her lap and crouches down in front of a potted peony. The slit on the back of her skirt opens and shows a bit of her red panties.

I walk to her and touch her arm with my paper. She jerks around and sees me. "Did you look for me?" she asks.

I smile. "It's not so hard to find you."

"It's cooler in here." She fumbles in her handbag and takes out a small envelope. She opens it and pulls out a papercut that looks like a fresh, juicy peach. "I cut Xuan paper and dyed it. The color is softer."

"It's so . . . appetizing." I put it at arm's length to peruse it. "I want to eat it." She giggles. A little embarrassed, I slide it back in the envelope and show her the red paper I brought. "I thought you might use this."

She holds the paper to her face, as if to smell it. "I'm beyond happiness."

There's a childlike joy on her face, which reminds me of my own daughters, Rou and Lian, who are far away raising families of their own. I wish I could share their burdens and happiness.

"My oldest daughter, who is your age, is expecting a baby."

She takes out a piece of red paper and folds it.

"What are you going to make?"

"A pomegranate. It has hundreds of tiny seeds, which stand for begetting many sons."

I watch her face. "What about a daughter? Can you cut me a peony?"

Her eyes freeze on the paper for a moment. "All right. A peony will bring you riches and prosperity." She borrows a pair of scissors at the counter.

She turns the paper to cut a long curve. "The round parts should be as round as the harvest moon, the points as sharp as a husk of wheat, the square parts as square as a brick, the spaces as clean as a saw's tooth, and the lines like whiskers."

"You have such nimble hands. Why do you want to tread the path of bad women?"

Her scissors stop, then resume cutting as she pulls the paper inside the blades. "I don't know what you're talking about, ma'am."

"You know what they advise a young woman—a single slip may cause lasting sorrow."

She drops the scissors and covers her face with her hands.

"Fortunately, life is not like papercutting. You can start over once or twice. But a woman's reputation is like a papercut. Once done, it's hard to fix."

"I came to Nanjing to have an abortion." Her shoulders

tremble. "I'm too ashamed to go home. I want to get a job and become a city resident."

I notice a clerk watching us and take Sui's elbow.

She winces. "I can't do this forever. Have mercy, please, don't bust me."

I whisper to her, "We can't talk here," and nudge her toward the ladies' room.

She pushes me aside. I collide into a column so hard that it takes me a half-minute to realize she's gone. We could've had a talk. I would've comforted her about the abortion she had and told her about the hysterectomy I must undertake. It's not easy to be a woman, old or young, and yet we can make the best of it. But she deserted me, because she was afraid and I was slow.

The clerk comes to me and asks, "Are you okay, ma'am?"

"Yes, I am." I stoop to lift the barely started peony from the floor.

"Is that your daughter?" she asks. "Young people have no manners nowadays."

"She's not my daughter." I show the clerk the longevity peach. "My daughters don't know how to do this." The papercut doesn't wither like a real fruit, so I can have it mounted and framed.

She tilts her head to study it. "I've seen lots of these at the crafts store, one yuan apiece."

"But I would've paid ten yuan, or more." I feel angry tears in my eyes. "What's money got to do with it?" Guanyin, the goddess of compassion, blesses a peony and the weeds by the roadside equally.

The clerk smiles and glances around the garden. "May I interest you in our specimen plants? Are you looking for anything in particular?"

"Yes." I fold the peony to put inside my handbag. "Do you still have those Old Faithful peonies? I'd like to buy a smaller pot, one that can be put on a hospital bed stand, because I'm going to have surgery."

"We do." She walks ahead, gesturing. "This way, ma'am."

A young woman passing me by holds a potted plant. I look back to see if she's Sui. She isn't, but I am not disappointed. One day we may meet again. I will ask her to finish cutting the peony, its soft ruffled petals opening to spread crimson joy after a long harsh winter.

ACKNOWLEDGMENTS

I thank the judges of the Juniper Prize and Edie Meidav for selecting my collection. Your writings opened my eyes and made me hungry for more. Thanks to the staff of the University of Massachusetts Press—Mary Dougherty, Sally Nichols, Courtney Andree, freelancer Dawn Potter, and everyone else—for your wonderful support. Thanks to my publicist, Leah Paulos, for helping my book reach its audience.

I thank my parents and Hai for sharing with me your lives, your stories, and your generous spirits.

I am beyond grateful to the teachers who helped me hone my craft and find my voice: Elizabeth Graver, Tom Bailey, Barbara Kingsolver, Elizabeth Evans, C. E. Poverman, Jonathan Penner, Robert Houston, and Christopher McIlroy. I thank the University of Arizona MFA program and my fellow writers for guiding me during the formative years of my writing career.

ACKNOWLEDGMENTS

To the editors of the following journals, where some of these stories first appeared, my thanks and appreciation:

Asian Pacific American Journal: "The Gourmet,"
"The Homely Girl"

Evansville Review: "My Old Faithful"

FUTURES: "Chimney," "Dream Lover," "The Homely Girl," "If You Were My Legend," "My Old Faithful," "The Umbrella"

Iconoclast: "Pining Yellow"

Nuvein Online: "The Match"

Porcupine Literary Arts Magazine: "The Birthday Girls"

Stories for Films: "Pining Yellow" (as a screenplay)

Finally, I want to thank Qin for your love and support. I couldn't have taken this path without you by my side. Forever and always, we live this adventure together.

JUNIPER
JUNIPER PRIZE FOR FICTION

This volume is the fourteenth recipient
of the Juniper Prize for Fiction,
established in 2004 by the
University of Massachusetts Press
in collaboration with the
UMass Amherst MFA Program
for Poets and Writers, to be
presented annually for an outstanding
work of literary fiction. Like its sister award,
the Juniper Prize for Poetry established
in 1976, the prize is named in honor
of Robert Francis (1901–1987),
who lived for many years at
Fort Juniper, Amherst, Massachusetts.